Ragged Heroes

By Andy Peloquin

Table of Contents

The Princelands

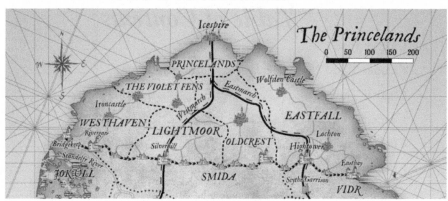

The Fehlan Wilds

Chapter One

"Keeper's beard, boy, you're one hell of an overgrown bastard!" Corporal Rold, a large man with a heavy black beard, dark eyes, and craggy face, shouted up at Endyn. "I've never seen a man so ugly a whore'd kick him out of bed, but blacken my boots, if you ain't the exception to the rule."

Duvain winced. Endyn bore the tirade with his usual stoic silence, but Duvain recognized the hardening around his brother's mouth, his typical response to the mockery he always drew.

The corporal's abuse continued unabated. "I'd say you have a face only a mother could love, but I can still see traces of the Keeper-damned raptor's egg you crawled out of." Though he didn't even reach Endyn's chest—few men did—his volume more than made up for the size difference. "Quite frankly, I'm sick just imagining the draconic-looking slit that managed to spew you out."

Duvain shifted and coughed. The movement drew the corporal's attention. "And you're not much better, shite-for-brains! Here I thought the big one was the ugliest of the lot, yet you look like some afterbirth disgorged from a demon's taint."

Duvain managed to keep the smile from his face. Corporal Rold's words rolled off him—his father had been particularly creative with his

1

insults after a few cups of agor. He'd learned to take the abuse; better he endure the stream of derision than letting Endyn, always an easy target, suffer under the shouts and stares of those who met him. Endyn's brutish exterior hid a kind, gentle soul.

"So you think you're good enough to join Onyx Battalion, eh?" Spittle flew from the corporal's mouth.

"No, sir!" Duvain responded at full volume, fighting the urge to wipe the moisture from his ear. "But we've been ordered to join the Ninth Company, and a good Legionnaire never questions orders." He thrust out the rolled up parchment that contained their instructions.

Corporal Rold looked at it as if at a leper's privates. With a disdainful expression, he took it, unrolled it, and scanned the contents with a disgusted grunt. "As if things weren't bad enough, now they're sending us the dreck of the army."

Duvain said nothing. He and Endyn had been at the bottom of their training company back in Voramis. They'd been lucky to be sent across the Frozen Sea to join the war against the Eirdkilrs at all.

"Bugger it!" Corporal Rold threw up his hands, rolling his eyes to the heavens. "At least they've given us a meat shield big enough to protect a few of us *real* Legionnaires from enemy arrows." He shot a glare at Endyn. "Not much good for much else, I wager."

Endyn's stiff posture and the hard set of his jaw spoke volumes. His right hand twitched at his side, the way it did when the dragonskin was driving him crazy. Duvain had no idea how his brother put up with the constant itching of the scaled, stiff, thickened patches of skin. The heavy mail shirts and breastplates had to be making the friction far worse. The dragonskin was one of the few things that could crack Endyn's stoicism.

"Get out of here!" The corporal gave a dismissive wave. "Owen here will show you where to stash your gear, then report back here for duty. Got it?"

"Yes, Corporal!" Endyn and Duvain shouted, giving their best salute.

2

With a snort and a muttered curse for "the fresh batch of incompetents", Rold strode off.

Private Owen, a sandy-haired Voramian with a weak chin and weaker shoulders made even narrower by his heavy armor, had stood behind the imposing corporal, listening to the tirade with a half-smile and a gleam in his grey eyes. Now, he stepped forward and extended a slim hand to Duvain. "Glad to meet you."

Duvain shook. He was surprised to find the private's hand strong and callused, despite its small size. "Duvain. This is my brother Endyn."

When Endyn shook, his huge hand—too large even on *his* massive frame—swallowed half of Owen's forearm. Owen tried hard not to show how much Endyn's height impressed him. Duvain had always been tall among the boys of Northfield, but Endyn stood at least head and shoulders above him, taller even than the huge warhorses roaming the camp. His brother had enormous shoulders and a barrel chest any blacksmith would envy, feet the size of a small coracle, and a patchy beard that concealed the outgrowths of skin that covered his oversized jaw. On the bad days, his dragonskin appeared above the neck of his gambeson. Thankfully, no trace of the grey rash-like growth was visible today.

"Don't mind the corporal," Owen told them. "He's a mean son of a bitch, no doubt about it, but a good one to have at your back in a fight. Stay out of his way, keep your hands out of his pack, and mind your shield, and he'll stick to just shouting at you."

Endyn and Duvain nodded. Endyn said nothing, but Duvain caught the tightness in his brother's expression. People tended to find an excuse to pick on Endyn, no matter what he did or didn't do. The fact that he stood nearly twice the height of the average man and, as Corporal Rold had taken pains to point out, had a face only his mother could love—had loved, with all her dearly departed heart—made him a target. He'd bear the abuse with his stoic silence until Duvain intervened. Intervention had earned him more than a few beatings, at least until Endyn realized his size gave him an advantage. None of the boys in Northfield had picked on either of them after Endyn waded into a few fights.

3

"This way," Owen said, nodding toward the muddy main avenue that cut through the heart of the encampment.

A city of tents, picket fences, and stables sprawled across the plains to the west of Icespire. The camp of the Legion of Heroes spread out over more acres than Duvain could count—roughly four thousand men were housed here at any given time, but the camp was sized for ten thousand soldiers. Plus the draft horses, oxen, carts, wagons, and teamsters that comprised the logistics trains delivering supplies around the conquered lands on the enormous island continent of Fehl.

Every Legion-issue canvas tent was identical: dun-colored square structures slightly taller than the average man, held up by ropes attached to iron stakes driven deep into the muddy ground. Despite the chaotic movement of men and animals in the camp, there was an orderliness that any architect would envy. The tents had all been erected in neat lines, with soldiers' and officers' tents surrounding the tents of their battalion commanders. As Owen explained, the soldiers were grouped by company and broken into platoons, with every eight to twelve-man squad occupying one of the huge tents.

The singular smell of "army camp" hung thick in the air. It was a distinct odor of dirt churned to muck by animal hooves and booted feet, sweaty men who bathed far too infrequently, and wet canvas and rope. Mud covered everything and everyone, painting the simple tents a dull, dusty grey. Men lounged in various states of undress, drank from pitchers and skins of every conceivable size and shape, and argued at full volume.

The Legion camp wasn't much to look at—certainly not the place of glory and heroism the recruiters had promised.

The city of Icespire, however, exceeded the fanciful descriptions of the men that had returned to Voramis. Duvain had spent his final hours on the boat watching the city drawing closer, the details of the city growing clearer.

Icespire derived its name from the single crystalline tower that rose from the highest point of the hill upon which the city sat. The tower reflected the blue of the ocean and the white of the fluffy clouds that clustered around the enormous structure. To Duvain, it seemed like a dagger of clear sapphire thrust by a giant's hand into the belly of the sky.

The city had grown up along the banks of the Frozen Sea, gradually expanding as more and more Einari—now called Princelanders—settled the land. Rivaling Voramis and Praamis back on the mainland, its denizens numbered well over four hundred thousand.

By comparison, the camp of the Legion of Heroes was small. Hard to believe that the army camp—a massive, sprawling thing that dominated the entire western slope of the hill—occupied enough farmland to raise crops for the entire village of Northfield.

Private Owen led them through the muddy lanes toward a tent that looked identical to the others around it. "This is us," he said, motioning for them to enter.

Duvain had to stoop to enter, but Endyn nearly bent double to fit through the opening. He remained hunched over—the peak of the tent barely cleared Duvain's head.

The slim private indicated the wooden two-level bunk bed in the front of the tent. "This'll be your bunk," he said. "Your packs get stowed beneath. The good news is that you won't have to worry about anyone filching your stuff. Sergeant Brash doesn't take kindly to that sort of thing. Last one who got caught with his hand in a comrade's pack…" He gave a wry grin. "Let's just say Brien had a mighty tough time scratching his behind for the next few weeks."

Duvain stashed his ruck—heavy after the long march from the dock—beneath the bunk and did the same with Endyn's.

He cast a glance up at his brother. "You good, Endyn?"

Endyn's eyes darted around the tent. Two pairs of bunk beds ran down each side of the tent. All were empty save for a grizzled man sitting on the bottom of the rearmost bunk. He paid them little heed—his focus was entirely on the leather wineskin in his hands.

Endyn nodded, his jaw clenched tight. Duvain knew his brother had an aversion to getting undressed with witnesses. He'd wait until he was alone.

Duvain removed the jar of unguent from his pack and set it on the top bunk, beneath the straw-stuffed pillow. "It's here if you need it."

5

"What's this, now?" A new voice greeted them. "Fresh meat, Owen?"

The newcomer that slunk into the tent was a shifty-eyed, rat-faced man with the wary, darting gaze of a career criminal. He walked on the balls of his feet, as if prepared to flee at a moment's notice. But the truly remarkable thing about him was his jewelry: a leather thong hanging around his neck, threaded with what looked like thick mushrooms. When Duvain got a closer look, he recoiled. They were human ears!

"Duvain and Endyn," Owen said. "Brothers, right?"

Duvain nodded.

Owen gestured. "This paragon of cleanliness is Weasel."

Weasel scowled. "Now, that ain't nice, Owen. We can't all go around smellin' of lavender and lilies like you."

Owen gave Weasel a grin. "Sure, but at least I've got the good sense to wash before *and* after I visit the ladies down at the Soldier's Rest. Minstrel knows I don't want *half* the diseases you've got."

"Better a diseased prick than a useless one, says I." Weasel gave a suggestive thrust of his hips. "Oh right, yer savin' yourself for the missus back home, ain'tcha?"

Owen's face hardened. "You know I am."

Weasel turned to Duvain and Endyn with a cruel grin. "Says he's got a wife back in Praamis waitin' for him. Knowin' the ladies like I do, I doubt very much she's doin' any sort of waitin'. Too much coin to be made in the right trade, if you catch my drift."

Owen's face reddened, and he opened his mouth to retort.

"Though, I very much doubt any missus exists at all!" Weasel continued before Owen got a word out. "I don't know no one here who can verify that particular claim. A lady back in Praamis, hah!" He shook his head. "Ain't nobody waitin' at home for any of us. It's why we came over here, innit?"

In Duvain and Endyn's case, Weasel wasn't far off. Their father and mother had died the year before—the Bloody Flux had claimed them, along with fully one third of their village of Northfield—leaving them with a barren tract of land they had no desire to farm. Dreams of a better life in the city of Voramis had called to them. Reality had been less kind. After a few weeks wasted in a fruitless search for work, with no coin to their name, they'd been wooed into the Legion of Heroes by a silver-tongued recruiter. The tales of glory and wealth held appeal—the promise of gold for their service and the spoils of war sold them on the idea. Six months of hard training, three weeks' march overland, another month on a ship, and a week of marching later, they had more than their fair share of sores and blisters. They hadn't seen gold or glory in all that time.

"Stop pissing with Owen, Weasel." The grizzled man at the back of the bunkhouse spoke for the first time. He threw the wineskin, now empty, aside and, standing, strode toward them. Grey showed at his temples and peppered his beard, and his face showed the signs of wear. A thick scar—either from sword or rope, Duvain didn't know—ran across his throat, hardening his voice to a harsh rasp. "You'll put him in a mood, and you know how our gruel will turn out when he's in a mood."

Owen's face brightened from a furious purple to a smug pink. "You never did guess what that *mystery* ingredient in yesterday's soup was, did you?"

Weasel turned an interesting shade of disgusted green. "If I find out you put somethin' in my food, I'll gut you like—Captain, sir!" He trailed off as a man entered the tent, his mouth clamping shut as he straightened and saluted. Owen and the grizzled man did likewise, Endyn and Duvain following suit a moment too late.

The captain was a tall, handsome man with broad shoulders, long blond hair tied back in a tail, and a serious face. He had a confident gait, and he moved with shoulders thrown back, head held high, and hand never far from his sword. A man of action and war, with the poise and self-assurance that only came through years of experience. Yet for all his professionalism, his eyes held none of the arrogance Duvain had found in other officers.

7

"So this is what they send me?" He studied the brothers. Duvain felt himself shrinking before those piercing green eyes. "Not a lot to work with, from what I hear."

Duvain snapped a salute. "Captain, we'll fight hard and work harder, sir!"

"Indeed." The captain stroked his smooth-shaven chin with a strong hand that bore no scars—a sign he knew his way around a sword. "It's all I can ask for, I suppose."

He turned his attention from Duvain up to Endyn. The big man tensed, his spine going rigid. Duvain didn't need to see his expression to know Endyn had grown nervous, no doubt expecting something derogatory from the captain, as he'd received from so many others in the past.

The captain only nodded. "You'll be a good addition to the ranks, once you're fully trained." He turned to the grizzled man. "Corporal Awr, drills at first light. Put the big one in the middle rank."

"Hewing spear, sir?" the corporal asked. "Shieldbreaker'll be too heavy, but I reckon a pig-sticker'd do the trick."

"Aye." The captain's eyes narrowed. He addressed Endyn. "Strong, but not too quick, am I right?"

Endyn colored, but nodded.

"There's no shame in it, soldier. We've all got our strengths." He held out his hand. "I trust you've got a good grip?"

Endyn took the captain's hand and squeezed, his massive forearm cording.

"You'll do, soldier." The captain turned back to Awr. "Anchor the formation on him, with the brother—" He shot a questioning glance at Duvain, who nodded. "—on his right. He'll need someone looking out for him. Once he gets the hang of the shield wall, he'll be a bloody hurricane."

"Aye, Captain." Corporal Awr snapped off a salute. The grizzled man treated the captain with a deference that struck Duvain as odd, given his previously taciturn demeanor.

"At ease, Corporal." The captain turned to Duvain and Endyn. "Welcome to the Deadheads, soldiers." With a nod, he turned and strode from the barracks.

As soon as he disappeared from sight, Owen and Weasel deflated. Owen let out a long breath. "No matter how many times I see him, I can't get over the fact that it's really *him*."

"Him?" Duvain asked.

"Captain Lingram." Weasel's brow furrowed. "Surely you've heard of him across the waters!"

Of course they had—everyone from Malandria in the north to Praamis in the east had heard of Captain Lingram, the Blacksword, Hero of Garrow's Canyon. He and a company of fewer than a hundred Legions had faced down four hundred Eirdkilrs in the canyon. The barbarians had hurled themselves against the Legionnaire's shields. Captain Lingram stood firm, refusing to give ground, intent on cutting off the enemy's advance into friendly territory. The captain had been one of the four men to walk out of that battle alive. Not a single Eirdkilr had survived. He'd received an honor from the King of Voramis and the Swords of the Princelands from Prince Toran of Icespire. Some had even whispered that he was being granted a patent of nobility.

"A shame what they've done to him." Owen shook his head. "He deserved better."

"What do you mean?" The tales of Lingram Blacksword had been filled with platitudes and honor; the private's words held a dark, dangerous undertone.

Owen frowned. "Captain Lingram should have been commander, even *general,* by now, but he's here stuck with the Deadheads."

"Some say he pissed in the wrong man's boots," Weasel said, shaking his head.

"Way I hear it, he slept with the wrong lordling's wife." Owen turned to the rat-faced man. "No wait, that was you."

Weasel grinned. "Nothin' I enjoy more than beddin' a noblewoman. There's somethin' wonderful about soilin' a fresh, clean—"

"Shut it, both of you twats!" Corporal Awr growled in his rasping voice. He fixed Duvain with a hard stare. "Captain Lingram stood up to a nobleman who was abusing his power. He took it upon himself to intervene when no one else would. He saved a man's life, and it cost him his career."

Weasel rolled his eyes. "No way you can know that, Awr. You're just a corpor—"

"I was there." The power in the man's quiet voice held more power than an ear-splitting shout. "He stood over the flogged man's body, sword in hand, facing down half the pissant lord's guards. Not a trace of fear in him, our Blacksword. He'd have fought and died, too, but the nobleman was too cowardly to cut him down. It wouldn't have gone over well, that sort of death."

Duvain exchanged glances with Endyn. This half of the story hadn't reached the mainland—he doubted it ever would.

"But that Keeper-accursed lordling has a father with just the wrong amount of influence on Fehl. One whisper in the wrong ears and Captain Lingram gets a shitty new demotion. That's how he ended up as head of our company, doing duties of a lieutenant." His face grew grim, dour. "No way he ever reaches commander now."

"Why not?" Duvain glanced at Owen, Weasel, and Awr in turn. "You've called the company Deadheads twice now. What's that mean?"

"Means we're the side of the Legion of Heroes you *don't* see in the parades, lad," Awr's voice was quiet, hard. "The kind they don't talk about when they're recruiting fresh-faced lads like you."

Duvain's forehead wrinkled in confusion.

"See that hideous necklace around Weasel's neck?" Awr motioned to the chain of ears. "He got most of those from the *wrong* barbies. Friendlies, the lot of them."

"How was I supposed to know?" Weasel asked, throwing up his hands. "They all look the same."

Awr scowled. "Owen here can't stand the sight of blood."

Owen colored. "Awr!" he protested.

Duvain raised an eyebrow.

Owen's red deepened in embarrassment. "I...I didn't know before I joined."

"Gets proper sick, he does." Weasel's grin broadened his face, making it even uglier. "Vomitin', shakes, the works."

Owen scowled. "At least—"

"I don't know what you did to get yourselves sent here," Awr continued, cutting off Owen with a scowl, "but it means you're one of us. You're a dreg." With a sneer, he shouldered past Duvain and out of the tent.

"Damn!" Weasel's eyebrows rose. "I ain't heard him speak that many words in months. Now you lot show up and he's talkin' like a bleedin' orator."

Owen rolled his eyes. "Anyways, that's the Deadheads for you."

"Seems like we'll fit right in," Duvain said with a smile.

"Meat!" Corporal Rold's harsh voice jarred Duvain to the bone. The corporal burst into the tent, glaring at them. "What in the bloody hell are you doing jack-jawing like a Blackfall doxy in a crowd of blind men? I said stow your gear and get your asses moving!"

"Sir, yes sir!" Duvain straightened, Endyn following suit.

"Ditch the sir sandwich, meat! It's Corporal, not 'sir yes sir'!"

"Yes, s—" Duvain swallowed. "Yes, Corporal! Gear's stowed, sir. Ready for duty."

"Good." Corporal Rold thrust a finger toward the open door. "You're off to do every soldier's favorite job. Owen, Weasel, seems like they need a couple of someones to show them the ropes."

"But Corporal—"

The bearded man loomed tall over the rat-faced soldier. "Not a word, Weasel, unless you'd rather do the job by yourself!"

Weasel's mouth snapped shut.

"Good," Rold snarled. "Now get the bloody hell out of here before I lose my patience."

Duvain noticed how Owen and Weasel gave the corporal a wide berth, and he determined to do likewise. Rold's eyes tracked Endyn as the big man shuffled from the room. A sinking feeling rose in the pit of Duvain's stomach. Rold had found a target, and Endyn would suffer.

* * *

Duvain fell to his knees, retching, emptying his meager rations into the span of muddy trench they'd just dug.

"Watcher's teeth! Not again!" Weasel grumbled. He leapt backward, out of range of Duvain's vomit. "Least you can do is point your spew the other way! These boots'll be hard enough to clean without your gettin' sick inside them."

Duvain wiped his mouth and staggered to his feet. His stomach was empty, but the foul smell of the latrine trenches twisted his stomach in knots. On his father's farm, he'd spent years mucking stables and hauling away horse and oxen droppings—this was far, far worse. The entire western half of the camp did their business in these latrine trenches. The meat-heavy diet of soldiers did little to reduce the stench of their meals on the way out.

Not for the first time, Duvain cast an envious glance at Endyn. His brother stood a short distance away, halfway through digging his own trench. They still had far too much ground to break before cutting off for the night. Endyn's strong arms made him the perfect candidate for hauling massive clumps of dirt in the wheelbarrow. He got to escape the trenches every once in a while, while Duvain was stuck down here, where the smell was overpowering enough to…

His stomach emptied again. Little more than watery acid came out.

"Keeper's taint," Weasel muttered. "Much more of that, and you'll start bringin' up blood."

"Duvain." Endyn's voice was clumsy. His thick tongue and heavy jaw struggled to form words, and they came out mangled. He rarely spoke because of it. "Here." He set the wheelbarrow down and reached for Duvain's shovel.

"No, Endyn." Duvain tried to tug the handle from his brother's massive hands—with less success than an infant tugging at a donkey's bridle. "I've got this."

Endyn fixed him with a stern glare and shook his head. "Go."

Duvain read the stubbornness in his brother's eyes. He'd never match Endyn's physical strength, but it was his brother's strength of will that was the true marvel. Endyn bore the burden of his dragonskin in near-silence, never complaining, rarely even admitting his pain or discomfort. Once his mind was made up, not even King Gavian himself could change Endyn's mind.

Concern filled his brother's expression. Duvain reddened, but Endyn's eyes bore no trace of accusation. Endyn's huge size and slowness had been one of the primary reasons they'd been sent to the Deadheads, but it was really Duvain's fault. Duvain had never been strong as a boy, and the illness that claimed his parents had left him weak. He could carry a shield and swing a sword, but more than a few minutes of effort left him exhausted. His stomach was weak, his senses too delicate for such potent smells. The army's training had pounded strength and stamina into him, but his muscles hadn't grown like Endyn's. He'd nearly been kicked out of the Legion—only Endyn's insistence and the demand for shields and swords had convinced their drill sergeant to send them across the Frozen Sea to Icespire and the legions stationed here.

Face burning, Duvain released his grip on the shovel handle and climbed out of the trenches. He gripped the wheelbarrow handles and pushed it toward the pile of dirt. He hated that his brother had to take care of him—Endyn had his own troubles to worry about. He'd thought joining the Legion would help him become strong. If anything, it had shown him how much he needed Endyn's help.

A man stood watching nearby, silent, his face hard. He wore a sergeant's uniform, and though he wasn't particularly large, there was something looming about him. Captain Lingram had been a large presence of confidence and concern, but this man radiated menace enough for a giant twice his size.

Duvain nodded as he passed, but had to fight back a shudder as he met the man's eyes. The eyes were cold—colder even than the Frozen Sea—with the dispassion of a reptile studying its prey.

He hurried to empty the wheelbarrow onto the growing mound of dirt and rushed back to the trench. The last thing he wanted was to see the anger or censure in those blue eyes. Those eyes held no approval or acceptance—they saw only weakness to be culled. The way the sergeant's gaze followed him, Duvain had no doubt *he* was the weakness that would be dealt with.

Chapter Two

From the slump of Endyn's shoulders and the weariness on his face, Duvain knew his brother was close to collapse. After hours of digging, Endyn moved stiffly; the dragonskin had to be getting to him, irritated by sweat and chafing beneath his heavy armor. Exhaustion would make things worse.

Duvain felt ready to collapse as well. They'd dug a latrine trench close to forty paces long, two paces deep, and six paces wide—military standard, according to Owen. He and Endyn had done enough digging on their father's farm to know their way around a shovel, but the work had left his back, arms, shoulders, and legs aching.

Owen and Weasel, however, showed little sign of fatigue.

"Quittin' time, lads!" With a cheery grin, Weasel thrust his shovel into the ground and spat into the trench. "Not bad for a first day of work. You embraced the suck as well as any recruit, I suppose."

Weasel glanced at Duvain. "You know what that means, don'tcha?" He held out a hand to help Duvain out of the trench. "Nothin' like a visit to The Old Wolf after a day like today. A drink'll sort you right out."

Duvain couldn't believe the man. Sweat soaked his tunic and the padding beneath his armor, and foul-smelling mud covered his legs, arms, face, and boots. Right now, he had no desire to do anything but bathe. Or sleep. No, bathe first, then sleep.

Owen shook his head. "I'd rather go someplace where beer is better than piss water. Besides, at The Old Wolf, you're more likely to get knifed or beaten than served a decent meal. Old Hartha hasn't cooked anything close to half-edible since his fifth decade. And he's pushing a hundred, easy."

Weasel shrugged. "Better than the chow they serve at the mess room." He shuddered.

"It's that bad?" Duvain asked.

Weasel's expression grew grim. "About the same as what me dearly departed mum used to make back in the Beggar's Quarter. Except she didn't shit in my food, like they do here." He glared at Owen.

"You took your chances when you pissed me off," Owen said with a satisfied grin. "Maybe you'll mind your mouth next time. Your lips are looser than a two-copper Praamian tart."

Weasel rolled his eyes. "Well, all that's said and done, time for us to be gettin' a drink." He turned to the brothers. "At least there's one good thing about this bleedin' cold: there's more'n enough ice to keep the drinks frosty."

For the first time, Duvain noticed the chill that had descended with the setting sun. A whistling wind carried cold through the camp, setting him shivering. A distinct smell of ice hung on the air.

"Gets bloody cold at night here." Owen said. "It's why we spend our time at The Old Wolf."

Weasel grinned. "Fightin' is always a good way to keep warm."

Duvain shot Endyn a glance. His brother's face was tight; he needed to get out of the armor and apply some of that salve before the dragonskin got too bad.

"Come on, lads!" Owen slapped Duvain's back. "First drink's on Weasel. Deadhead tradition."

"Hey now!" Weasel protested. "That ain't fair—"

"Run your mouth a bit faster next time, and you won't be stuck with the tab." Owen grinned.

Grumbling, Weasel motioned for them to follow.

Owen explained on the way. "First drink of the night's always on the last man to call it. Though, knowing Weasel, he'll end up taking a few coins from one of the other companies. Man hasn't paid for his own ale since the day I met him. It's why we always make sure he's stuck with the tab." He studied Duvain. "You get your first pay, yet?"

Duvain shook his head. "They said we get it after our first week."

"Bloody money-grubbin' pricks," Weasel growled. "We didn't get paid until after the first month."

Owen rolled his eyes. "You'd think with all the riches we're pulling out of these hills, the cake-eating powers that be would be a bit happier to fork over our rightful pay."

Duvain's eyebrows rose. "Riches?"

"Ah, right," Weasel sneered. "I forget you all back across the sea only hear the rosy side of things."

Owen's face fell. "Weasel, that's not—"

"Don't let *this one*"—Weasel jerked a thumb at Owen—"tell you this war had anythin' to do with Prince and country. For some, like him, it may be good and well to serve for patriotism, but that ain't the reason most of us are here. Especially not the ones at the top."

His rat-like face darkened. "There's gold in those hills. A bleedin' lot of it. Enough to fill every bathtub in Voramis, Praamis, and Malandria and then some. Silver, too, along with plenty of precious stones. All of which our gracious hosts of Icespire are itchin' to get their hands on."

Duvain exchanged a glance with Endyn. His brother's face mirrored his own surprise. The tales of glory and honor fighting to protect Einan from the savage Eirdkilrs hadn't included any mention of riches.

Weasel snorted. "Half the gold flowin' around the south of Einan has come from these hills. It's what brought us Einari here in the first place, five hundred years ago."

Duvain's brow furrowed. "I thought we came to punish the raiders that tried to invade Einan."

Owen inclined his head. "Aye, there's a bit of that, as well. The Fehlan raiders pissed off the wrong people back when, so they sent an army first to wipe out their ships, then invade their land. But some lucky bastard found himself lost in a mountain filled with gold, and that's when muckety-mucks decided the land of Fehl needed a bit of civilization. They started a settlement here and kept shipping more and more men across the water. Eventually, the settlement grew into a city, which became what we know as the city of Icespire."

Duvain cast a glance back. The glassy surface of Icespire itself caught the fading rays of sunlight, gleaming in myriad hues of orange, red, and purple.

Owen continued. "The bigger the city grew, the more us Einari kept coming and taking more land from the Fehlans. That's when the gold really started flowing. And would have kept on flowing, had the Eirdkilrs not decided they'd had enough of us."

Everyone in the south of Einan knew the grisly tales of the Eirdkilrs, a massive tribe of barbarians that lived in the deep, winter-laden south of Fehl. No one had ever seen where they came from, but they outnumbered the other barbarian tribes that lived north of the Sawtooth Mountains. Anyone brave or foolish enough to travel south beyond the mountain range never returned.

"When they decided it was time for us to give them their land back, they started coming through the Sawtooth Mountains and pushing back the small colonies and settlements established. That's when the lords of Icespire called for help from the big cities on Einan."

Malandria, Praamis, and Voramis were the main cities to send armies across the ocean, but many smaller cities had joined in the fight as well. *Not* for patriotism or colonization, it seemed.

18

Weasel shook his head. "The Eirdkilrs wanted to charge the Icespire lords more for the gold than they was willin' to pay. The noblemen decided it was easier to pay soldiers and mercenaries than the savages. Thus, we find ourselves on this glorious side of the world, along with all the other sods too dumb, ugly, or useless to find other employment."

"You speak so kindly of yourself," Owen chuckled.

Weasel shrugged. "I know what I am and what I ain't. I never had a problem with my role in things. Here, I get paid to do what I woulda done back home. Except I ain't fightin' in a gang on the streets of Praamis. Though, given this bloody freeze, I'm almost tempted to go back to that life. Hunger ain't nothin' compared to the Keeper-damned cold."

Duvain glanced at Endyn. As expected, his brother had pulled his cloak tighter against the chill. Endyn's dragonskin was sensitive to the chill, which only made things worse. He couldn't get out of his clothes to relieve the terrible itching, but the more he bundled up, the more the sweat added to his discomfort. Endyn's jaw was clenched tight; his brother was suffering, and there wasn't a thing he could do about it.

Not much the healers at the Sanctuary could do either. They'd tried all manner of salves, unguents, and potions to treat the strange rash they called dragonskin. One had even called in a Secret Keeper, who'd poked and prodded at the flaking, crusted patches of skin in silence for an hour before shrugging and walking out. The Ministrants had given Endyn a salve that reduced the itching and soothed some of the irritation, but did little for the hardening. On the bad days, Endyn could hardly move for the thick scales covering his chest, shoulders, and arms.

And that was just the rash. The healers hadn't found an explanation for Endyn's abnormal growth either. He'd been born the same size as any of the other Northfield kids—or so his mother had said—but by his tenth birthday, he'd been taller than both their parents. Endyn grew and kept on growing until his father had no choice but to build a special, oversized room in the barn. He and Duvain had lived there until the day they left home, with only each other and the animals for company.

That had saved them when the Bloody Flux hit, or so the Bloody Minstrel priests had said. The Trouveres had droned on about evading most of the noxious vapors of death that swept through their house. Duvain had caught a bit of the Flux, the cause of his weakness, but the priests had insisted they were blessed to have survived when their mother, father, and so many others of Northfield succumbed.

Even though Duvain recovered from the Flux, Endyn's sicknesses had never been explained. No one had found a cure or treatment. Though he tried not to show how much it bothered him, Duvain knew his brother well enough to recognize the signs. Endyn wanted to go and rest, but he wouldn't show his discomfort. They had already been relegated to the Deadheads, the dregs of the Legion of Heroes, because of Endyn's strange conditions and Duvain's weakness.

The sea of tents ended, and beyond stood the only proper structure Duvain had seen outside Icespire. The Old Wolf was aptly named: the wooden building had faded and gone grey, fraying around the edges, with a tired look. Hard-drinking soldiers caused the sort of damage no tavernkeeper could ever fully repair. The roof wouldn't survive the heavy winter, not the way it sagged beneath the weight of its thatch.

A tumult of shouts and laughter echoed within the tavern, but a handful of Legionnaires stood outside, drinking in the cool, night air rather than suffer the stale, stinking reek of sweating men, vomit, and yeasty ale.

"Here we are, lads!" Weasel gestured toward the tavern. "Best ale in camp."

"Only ale in camp," Owen whispered. "At least legally."

One of the Legionnaires, a tall, broad-shouldered man with dark eyes and a jawline that could cut diamonds, stepped forward and thrust out a hand to bar their progress. "Not a bloody chance, Deadheads. Not when you smell as bad as you look."

Another man, slimmer, with angular features, narrow shoulders, and bright scarlet hair, snickered behind him. "There's a pig trough

20

around the back of the tavern. I might be able to convince the tavernkeeper to pour some ale in there for you."

Weasel shot the red-haired man a rude gesture. "Get bent, Rynale!" He squared up with the other Legionnaire, uncaring that the man towered over him. He gave a little sniff and a theatrical groan. "You don't smell much better yourself, Addyn."

"Ooh, good insult." Addyn laughed. "You'll have to get a bit more creative if you want to get past me." His eyebrows rose as his eyes fell on Endyn. "Bloody hells, Weasel! You found yourself an ogre roaming the mountains, did you?"

Endyn's face hardened.

"No," Duvain stepped forward. "In your mother's bed. Said he was the best lover she'd had since your uncle-father."

Addyn's face darkened. "Little puppy's got some bark on him, does he?" He moved around Weasel to stare down at Duvain. "What's your name, meat?"

"Your father," Duvain snapped. Behind him, Endyn chuckled, a low, rumbling sound that resembled a half-growl.

Addyn's fists clenched, but Endyn stepped forward to loom behind Duvain. Addyn studied Endyn, as if sizing him up.

"If you don't mind," Owen said, interposing himself between Duvain and Addyn, "we'll just get our ale and be on our way."

"Not smelling like that, you won't," Rynale sneered.

Owen shot the man a sweet smile. "You put in a hard day's work sometime, Rynale, and maybe you'll find out what it means to be a *real* man."

A third Legionnaire, this one not quite as tall or wide as Addyn, snorted. "Seems like you real men are busy mucking around in shite, while us little nobodies get to do all the fighting." He shook his head, tsking. "It's an unfair world we live in. I know I'd love nothing more than latrine duty."

21

"You'll get your chance," Weasel retorted. "Now step aside before I set my *ogre* here to rearrange your spinal column. I'd say havin' your head shoved up your ass could improve your looks significantly."

Endyn loomed over Addyn. Despite his height, the Legionnaire barely reached Endyn's chest. Endyn flexed one huge fist, the size of Addyn's head.

"Bah!" Addyn stepped aside, pinching his nose. "I doubt the place could get any worse than it already has. Third Platoon is in there, and you know what that means."

Weasel rolled his eyes. "Aye, the dog-buggers are wavin' their pricks around like they know their business."

Addyn snorted. "All they know to do is stick their fingers in their bungholes. I'll bet even *Owen* here could figure that out."

Owen colored and bristled, but Addyn gave a dismissive wave. "Enjoy your ale, Deadheads. And keep the big one on a leash. He gets too much liquor in him, he's likely to collapse and crush half a dozen men." With a one-fingered salute, he turned back to his drink and his squad.

Weasel hustled them toward the door, where a crowd of men stood between them and their drinks. The little rat-faced Legionnaire slipped through the press of people with the expertise of a thief in a crowd. Heads turned toward them as Endyn ducked beneath the lintel. When he stood, his head nearly scraped the wooden ceiling beams. Men gave way for him, and all eyes followed his progress toward the bar.

Duvain read tension in Endyn's shoulders, his stiff spine. His brother had no desire to be the center of attention—he'd drawn stares since his fifth birthday. Endyn wanted to be normal, not the freak of nature people had believed him to be for so long.

Corporal Rold sat at the bar, a tankard of ale clutched in his hands. Despite the crush of Legionnaires, there was an empty chair on either side of the corporal. Perhaps the dagger driven into the wooden bar top had something to do with that. The tavernkeeper shot nervous glances at the blade every time he hustled past, but said nothing.

The storm brewing in Rold's eyes swelled to a full blown gale as he saw them approach. "Piss off, the lot of you. Only real men drink here."

"Real man, reportin' for duty!" Weasel snapped off a mocking salute. "Tavernkeeper, four of your finest ales. On me." With a wink, he hefted a purse.

"You didn't!" Owen groaned.

Weasel shrugged. "He was the one stupid enough to get within liftin' distance of me. Second Platoon ought to know better by now. If Addyn's pockets end up bein' a few imperials lighter, it will teach him to be more cautious of his belongin's."

Four tankards of ale arrived a few moments later, filled to the brim, with a thick layer of froth. Duvain hesitated a moment before taking a sip. The potent taste—a mixture of malted barley, yeast, juniper berries, and herbs he'd never tasted before—set him coughing. Weasel and Owen laughed, and even Endyn smiled.

Duvain scowled, which only made the two Legionnaires laugh harder. He'd never been much for ale—he'd prefer a good Voramian wine or Nyslian brandy, on the rare occasions he'd managed to scrape together enough coin to buy it. He knew better than to order such "woman's shite" at a Legionnaire's bar. He'd gotten his bollocks kicked in the last time he'd made that mistake.

Gritting his teeth against the syrupy brew, he forced himself to swallow. Thankfully, Endyn emptied his tankard in a few quick gulps, and Duvain could pour the rest of his into his brother's mug while Owen and Weasel drank deep from theirs. Drinking was one of the few ways to bond with one's fellow comrades—rejecting a drink was paramount to spitting in a fellow Legionnaire's face.

"You bastard!" A furious roar cut through the commotion in the tavern. The raucous conversations died, and all eyes turned toward the door.

"Crap," Weasel muttered, and drained the last of his tankard.

Duvain turned to see Addyn stalking toward them, his face flushed in anger, fists clenched. "You weasel-faced bastard!" The Legionnaire stabbed a finger at Weasel. "You bloody stole my purse."

"I did no such thing!" Weasel proved a superb actor. He managed to look both offended and outraged, with a hint of dignified mixed in. "If anythin', I *saved* your purse! I saw it lyin' on the ground, and I thought to myself, 'I can't let my good friend Addyn's coin be stolen by a lowlife.' So I picked it up and brought it here for safekeepin'." He dropped the purse into Addyn's hand. "And now it's safe."

Addyn opened it, his scowl deepening. "There's coins missing."

"Damned thieves!" Weasel muttered, angry. "I'll be sure to speak to my sergeant in the mornin', and we'll get to the bottom of this first thing in the—"

Addyn's fist was a blur in the lamplight. It connected with Weasel's jaw, a meaty *thump* that echoed through the room. The impact rocked Weasel's head back, where it bounced off the wooden bar. The little man sagged and didn't get up.

Addyn leaned over the unconscious man. "That'll teach you, you thieving bastard!"

Rold went from hunched over his mug to on the attack in an instant. His knee came up into Addyn's face, snapping the Legionnaire's head up. He drove his fist into Addyn's gut and swung his elbow around into the side of his head. Addyn followed Weasel to the floor.

"He's *our* thieving bastard!" Rold snarled down at the fallen Legionnaire.

Addyn lay on the filthy bar floor, his eyes glassy and unfocused. After a moment of stunned silence, Rynale and the other man shouted and charged, fists swinging.

For the first time, the perpetual frown on Rold's face disappeared, replaced by a hint of a smile. The sort of smile a cat gives to a mouse trapped between its paws. Duvain had known many boys and men like Rold—he and Endyn had been their targets all their lives. The corporal *wanted* the fight. It gave him an excuse to hurt others.

Roaring in laughter, Rold squared off and met the two charging men. He turned aside Rynale's punch and drew back his fist to answer with his own, but the other man went low, arms encircling his waist. Rold was slammed backward into the wooden bar counter with bone-jarring force. The two Legionnaires went down to the ground in a heap of tangled limbs and cracking wooden stools.

Rynale drew back to kick at the prone Rold, but Owen's boot caught him in the fork of the legs. The red-haired Legionnaire went down hard. Another man wearing the same company insignia charged, catching Owen in a grapple. Before Owen could break free of his attacker, a third and fourth Legionnaire rushed to join the fight.

Duvain knew he had to act. He'd never been much of a fighter, but he'd learned the basics of unarmed combat—hammered into him by the ruthless drill sergeant at basic training. He'd pounded at the straw dummies until his lungs burned and his fists bled. He stepped in the path of the oncoming Legionnaires and lashed out with a right cross at one man's jaw.

The problem with fighting men instead of dummies—one he'd failed to anticipate—was that real men fought back. His blow barely fazed the man, who answered with a punch of his own. Duvain ducked beneath the powerful swing, only to be caught in the chest by the second strike. Without his armor—they'd left it in the barracks before heading off to the bar—he had nothing but a thin tunic to take the punishment. The impact drove the wind from his lungs and he fell back against the bar, wheezing.

With a savage grin, the Legionnaire drew back his fist to finish Duvain. A massive shadow loomed over the man, and Endyn's hand engulfed his forearm. Barely grunting with the effort, Endyn lifted the man from his feet and hurled him across the bar, where he crashed to the ground and rolled into a table. The sound of shattering crockery and clattering metal tankards was followed a moment later by a furious roar of rage.

A new figure stalked toward them. Stocky, bearded, with a scarred face and a voice harder than granite, the man wore a sergeant's colors. An inferno raged in his eyes. "You spilled my drink, you poxy wankers!" He strode toward Endyn and stared up at him. "Are *you* the one responsible?"

Endyn didn't have time to react before the sergeant attacked. He drove a fist into Endyn's gut, doubling him over. Duvain winced as the following uppercut caught his brother under the chin.

Endyn staggered and caught himself against the bar, blinking hard. Shaking his head, he regained his feet and kicked out. His huge boot caught the sergeant in the gut. The force of the blow lifted him from his feet and hurled him backward. His falling body bowled over three more men rushing to join the fight.

"Enough!" The single word, loud and harsh, cut through the din. All eyes turned toward the door.

The man Duvain had seen earlier stood there. His eyes held no anger—they held nothing at all. They were ice cold, lifeless, like a walking corpse. The crowd of Legionnaires gave way before him as he strode toward them.

"Sergeant Brash, sir!" Owen managed to choke past the arm encircling his throat. The man holding him immediately released his grip and stepped out of the way. Owen snapped off a salute, wincing as he swallowed.

Rold staggered upright, one opponent unconscious at his feet and facing off against two more. At Owen's words, he whirled toward the sergeant and mirrored the salute—an action made difficult by the way he hunched over his left side.

Duvain helped Endyn to stand. His brother wobbled but stayed upright.

The sergeant who'd attacked Endyn strode toward them. "Sergeant Brash, get your dogs under control!" He wiped blood from the corner of his mouth. "If you don't, *I* will."

Brash regarded the man. "Sergeant Chaol." He said nothing else, simply met the man's glare. The two sergeants squared off, their eyes locked on each other. An unspoken war of wills passed between the two of them.

26

After a moment, both nodded. "Deadheads," Sergeant Brash called out, not taking his eyes from Sergeant Chaol. "To your barracks, double time."

"Yes, Sergeant!" Owen struggled to lift Weasel's unconscious form.

Duvain slipped Weasel's arm over his shoulder and, together, they dragged the limp man from the tavern.

Duvain cast a worried glance up at Endyn. Blood trickled from Endyn's massive mouth, and a bruise was already forming underneath his jaw. That would hurt like hell in the morning.

"Damn, Endyn!" Owen whistled softly as they hustled up the muddy alley toward their tent. "You just knocked Sergeant Chaol on his ass. Not many in camp can say the same. You're a good piece of gear." He nodded to Duvain. "The both of you."

Endyn said nothing, but a ghost of a smile appeared. Duvain grinned and adjusted his grip on Weasel's arm. "Will he be all right?" The unconscious man had begun to come to, though he did little more than mutter incoherently.

Owen nodded. "Weasel's taken more than his fair share of knocks. He'll hurt bad in the morning, but serves him right for messing with Addyn and the rest of Chaol's crew."

Duvain chuckled, but it made his chest hurt. The effort of hauling Weasel set him wheezing. He'd do his own share of hurting the following day.

They reached their tent and deposited the still mumbling Weasel into his bed. The grizzled corporal, Awr, filled the night with his heavy breathing, another empty wineskin hanging limp from his hand. With a wink, Rold muttered about "seeing a woman about a stiff flagpole" and disappeared. Owen excused himself to find some water and wash up before getting to bed.

The prospect of a bath sounded glorious, but the long morning of marching, the afternoon of digging, and the night's skirmish had left him exhausted. Endyn's fatigue mirrored his own.

"How bad is it?" Duvain asked.

Endyn shook his head. "Little bit," he said in his thick, heavy voice.

"Strip down. Let me take a look."

After a moment of hesitation, Endyn removed his tunic.

Duvain winced. Thick, grey scales covered Endyn's broad back, with red, inflamed cracks throughout. Dragonskin, a condition for which the Ministrants at the Sanctuary in Voramis had found no cure. The scales had thickened, grown harder to the touch. They made an eerie *clicking* as Endyn's movements rubbed them together.

Duvain strode around Endyn, examining the scales. They'd first appeared on his back, but soon spread along his sides, up his chest, and down across his stomach. Judging by the stiffness of Endyn's posture, the scales had reached his legs.

"Damn it, Endyn, this is bad!"

His brother shrugged huge shoulders, but sorrow filled his eyes.

Duvain dug under his pillow and produced the jar of unguent. "I'll put some on now, but I *have* to apply it again in the morning if you don't want it to keep getting worse." The salve—a fragrant mixture of rose hips, milk thistle, ground oats, aloe leaf, mint leaves, chamomile, slippery elm, and evening primrose oil—soothed Endyn's skin and softened the scales. But nothing could slow the growth. Eventually, the scales would completely cover Endyn's body. Duvain didn't know how long his brother had left—it could be months or years—but the dragonskin would someday kill him.

Not if Duvain had a say in it. He'd do everything in his power to keep that day at bay. With a heavy heart, he opened the jar of salve and began the arduous process of applying it to Endyn's huge back, sides, and chest. Endyn was the only family he had left; he couldn't lose him, too.

Chapter Three

"Keeper take you!" Weasel shouted up at Endyn, rubbing the back of his head. "First you keep me up last night with your abominable snorin', then you stink up the barracks, now you can't stop swingin' that spear around like you're showin' off your prick for a line of whores. If we were in proper battle, you'd have killed me a dozen times over, and not a single bastard barbarian dead!"

Endyn colored and hung his head. He hadn't slept well—the dragonskin made him uncomfortable no matter what position he slept in—and the ruck march had left him exhausted. Now, he struggled to master the unfamiliar hewing spear. The forearm-long blade was heavier than a typical spear, and though his muscles could handle it without difficulty, the odd balance threw him off.

Duvain wanted to stand up for his brother, but the look in Endyn's eyes told him to keep his mouth shut. His own performance in the battle line made Endyn's seem coordinated. He'd crunched the toes of the men behind him, stumbled into Corporal Awr on his right, and knocked Endyn's spear arm wide of a measured thrust. Once, he'd actually managed to drop both his spear and the long, rectangular shield issued to every Legionnaire. And *he* had been the one to nearly decapitate Weasel.

"Again, Sergeant!" Captain Lingram shouted. The captain sat atop his horse a short distance away, his eyes narrowed in concentration as he watched his company perform maneuvers. People as far away as Voramis could see his displeasure.

"Keep it forward, Endyn," Owen said from behind them. "Weapon toward the enemy at all times."

"Hewin' spear like that'll lop a head off," Weasel snarled. "Just make sure it ain't mine."

Duvain adjusted his grip on his spear and raised his shield. The sergeant had positioned him and Endyn in the third row. The two front ranks held the enemy at bay with shields and short swords, while the third and fourth rows used long spears to strike at the enemy. They were the foremost offensive line, but all they'd accomplished was to butcher their formation in all the wrong ways.

As Sergeant Brash called the maneuver again, Duvain desperately tried to move in step with the men behind, ahead, and beside him. He stumbled but caught himself before he toppled into Awr. The grizzled corporal shot him a venomous look, menacing despite his red-rimmed, bleary eyes. Awr winced with every barked command, every clank of their mail and breastplate. Duvain didn't envy him—he'd spent one agonizing hour training while hungover and determined never to do it again.

With a shout, Weasel dropped his weapons and whirled on Endyn. "That's it! I've had enough of your damned fumblin'. "

"Sorry," Endyn rumbled.

"Sorry ain't going to cut it when I get a barbarian arrow in my face because you're too stupid and clumsy to keep the formation." Weasel's face darkened to a furious purple.

"Private Cerlin!" Sergeant Brash's voice cracked like a whip. "That's enough."

Weasel's jaw worked. He turned to Captain Lingram. "All due respect, Captain, but this one's just goin' to get us all killed! He'll do as an arrow magnet, but not a whole Keeper-damned lot more."

"Silence, Private." Captain Lingram dismounted and strode through the parting ranks of Legionnaires toward them. "Are you trying to tell me you were a lot more competent on your first day in drills?"

Weasel reddened. "Sure, but not as bad as—"

"The Legion of Heroes is more than just an army, Private. It's a group of individuals fighting a common enemy, striving to achieve the same goal. Do you know what that goal is, Private?"

"To survive, Captain." Weasel swallowed. "And with him at my back, I don't see much chance of that happenin'."

Captain Lingram's face hardened. "Private, in my years of service, I've learned that you should *never* discount the man at your back. They may be the only thing standing between you and certain death when the time comes."

Weasel, finally, kept his mouth shut.

The captain met the little man's gaze. "You say he's rubbish at holding the line? Perhaps it's because no one took the time to think about how hard it is for *him* to hold a line organized for men half his size." He turned to Endyn. "With a bit more room, you think you can manage?"

Endyn hesitated, then nodded. "Yes, Captain."

"Good," Captain Lingram said. His eyes came to Duvain. "You're the shield guarding his weapon arm, but give him a bit of room to swing." He moved Duvain a single step to the right. "Keep your shield close, but not so close he can't move."

He strode around Endyn and moved the Legionnaire on the far side a single step away. "In proper formation, this space would be filled by two men." He winked at Endyn. "Seems like you're big enough for two of us, eh?"

Endyn grinned. "Yes, Captain," he rumbled.

With a nod, Captain Lingram strode back to his horse and swung up into the saddle. "Again, Sergeant Brash."

31

"Company, move!"

$$* * *$$

"Well I'll be damned." Weasel dumped the ladle of water over his face. "Turns out the two of you ain't as useless as you seem."

Owen frowned. "I remember you being a pretty pathetic Legionnaire your first day, Weasel. Hell, even now, you're about as useful as a sack of smashed eggs."

Weasel scowled, bringing a laugh to Owen's face.

"Chuckle it up, fools," Rold snapped. The corporal stood a short distance away. His perpetual scowl had returned. "When they're the ones who get you killed in the battle line, you won't be cracking jokes."

"Give them time, Rold," Owen protested. "They've been here one day. If their drill sergeants were anything like mine, they were more concerned about breaking their spirits than actually getting them ready for war." He dropped his voice to a mutter. "Almost reminds me of you."

"I heard that, you poxy runt." Rold's scowl deepened, and Owen took an instinctive step back. "And if the captain wasn't sitting over there, I'd stick my foot up your ass and wear you around the camp like the world's ugliest, dumbest sandal."

Owen's face tightened. He turned back to Duvain and Endyn. "Look, you two aren't all that great in a fight just yet, but you've got time. We're the Deadheads—we're not going to battle any time soon."

The high, ringing sound of a horn reverberated through the camp. All of them glanced toward the entrance to the training ground. A rider galloped across the barren field, horse kicking up clods of dirt churned to mud by their boots. He reined in before Captain Lingram. Though Duvain couldn't hear the brief exchange, he caught a glimpse of white as the messenger took a scroll from his pouch and handed it to the captain. With a salute, he rode off.

"That can't be good," Rold muttered.

Duvain followed Rold, Owen, and Weasel toward the captain. Awr stood beside Captain Lingram, engaged in a quiet conversation.

"I don't like it," Corporal Awr was saying.

"We've our orders, Corporal." Captain Lingram's voice held an odd tightness, and a new tension lined his face. "Ours not to question."

"Aye, Captain." Awr snapped a salute.

The captain raised his voice to address them all. "Ninth Company, we have been given marching orders."

A worm of anxiety squirmed in Duvain's gut. He'd expected their company, the Deadheads, the dregs of the Legion of Heroes, would remain in camp. But the captain's face told a different story.

Captain Lingram held up the parchment. "Onyx Battalion is to reinforce our troops at Dagger Garrison, and that includes us."

Duvain's gut clenched. They were going so close to the front line? He wanted to vomit.

Captain Lingram held up a finger. "We move out within the hour. Check your gear, break down your tents, and prepare to march. We have been summoned, men, and we will answer the call to arms." With a salute, he mounted his horse and trotted off the field.

For a moment, none of the men of Ninth Company moved. They exchanged glances, as if struggling to believe their ears.

"You heard the captain!" Sergeant Brash's words, eerily quiet and calm, broke the silence. "One hour, lads. Be ready." He didn't need to shout; the assurance in his voice had enough effect. The knots of men rushed toward their tents to break camp.

"Get a move on, meat!" Rold shoved Duvain toward the encampment. "We've our marching orders. Any thought of desertion, and I'll string you up by your innards, got it?" The look in Rold's eyes made it clear: the corporal would *enjoy* carrying out his threat.

Duvain nodded. "You've nothing to fear from us. We're Legionnaires, just like you." He only wished his voice didn't quaver so much, or that he felt a fraction as confident as he tried to sound.

* * *

Duvain's pack weighed twice as much as it ought to. He couldn't get the straps to sit on his shoulders right, and it felt as if it would drag him backward. During basic training, he'd gone on enough ruck marches to know not to expect a featherweight load, but this was too much. How could they possibly expect him to haul such a heavy pack and march all day long?

Endyn actually groaned as he struggled to slip his arms through the straps of his oversized pack. The dragonskin made his movements stiff and clumsy, and the heavy ruck would rub the scales raw.

"Is it bad?" Duvain asked.

Endyn hesitated, his jaw tight, and gave a half-hearted shrug.

Duvain fumbled at his pack's drawstring. "We've got time to apply a bit of the salve before—"

"Move it, you hedge-born yokels!" Rold's voice appeared in the tent a moment before his bearded face. "The other companies are already in line, and you two are dawdling like a pair of moonstruck milkmaids."

Endyn met Duvain's gaze. Though his brother's face was stony, pain filled the big man's eyes. "Let's go," he rumbled. There was no helping it. Endyn would have to tough it out until they had a chance to rest.

Groaning beneath the burden of their packs, they hurried after Rold. All around them, the soldiers of Onyx Battalion hastened to tear down their tents, stow their equipment, and don armor. The men moved with the speed of practiced experience. Less than an hour had passed since the captain gave orders to move, and already a long line of

Legionnaires streamed toward the companies waiting on the road, following him through the camp.

The Legion of Heroes was on the move.

Ninth Company held position at the rear of a league-long column of men, horses, and wagons. The Deadheads, the men of the company's Third Platoon, stood at the back.

Rold shoved Duvain into place behind Owen. "You and the arrow-magnet," he nodded to Endyn, "go here, where I can keep an eye on you." He lowered his voice. "Keep the pace, keep your mouth shut, and we'll get through the day fine."

Duvain cast a glance at the sky. The sun had reached its peak—they had at least five hours of marching before calling a halt to rest. Days this far south in Fehl were longer than on the mainland, and the nights shorter.

"How far is Dagger Garrison?" he asked Owen.

"Not sure," the Legionnaire answered without turning his head. "Six, maybe seven hundred miles. Cavalry'd get there faster, but us dust-eaters got no choice but to hoof it."

"Pleasant enough day for a walk, though," Weasel said, humor in his voice. "I figure this little jaunt is as good a hump as you're goin' to get until you make it home to that pretty imaginary girl of yours, Owen."

Duvain didn't catch Owen's retort, but his middle finger salute conveyed the message.

Sergeant Brash marched down the line, inspecting the men and their gear. He tightened the strap on Owen's pack and snapped an order for Weasel to tighten the laces on his boots. When he reached Endyn, he gave him a cold-eyed stare. "You slow us down, we'll cut you loose. Got it?"

Endyn nodded. "Yes, Sergeant," he rumbled.

The sergeant's gaze shifted to Duvain. "Goes for you, too. You're a Legionnaire now, so act like it. Long day's march ahead of us, but if you

35

get tired, I'm sure the corporal here will be happy to give you a cup of suck it the fuck up."

Duvain snapped a salute. "Yes, Sergeant!" He caught himself before saying "sir" again.

Sergeant Brash's face didn't change. He moved on without a word.

Rold snorted. "Whatever you do, do not piss the sergeant off. Especially after last night."

"You mean the fight *you* started?" Duvain asked.

He felt Rold's glare burn into the back of his neck. "You've Weasel to thank for that. I just stood up for our company."

Weasel snorted. "Bull-shite! You're just an ornery bastard who likes to fight."

"You'll be glad for that when I save your hide on the battlefield," Rold retorted. "Maybe next time, I'll leave you to be pummeled so you'll remember it."

Weasel's reply was cut off by Sergeant Brash's booming shout. "Company, march!"

* * *

Two hours into the march, and Duvain couldn't wait for the day to be over. His lungs burned and his legs ached despite the slow, steady pace across the flatlands south of Icespire. The straps of his pack dug into his shoulders. He wanted nothing more than to cast off his pack and run free of its burden. Only Rold's presence at his back—and the nervous fear of what the corporal would do if he slowed down their company—kept him moving.

According to Owen, they'd be expected to cover at least twenty miles to reach their campsite before nightfall. At this rate, Duvain felt as if his feet would be worn to the nub by the time they stopped. He couldn't begin to imagine how painful everything would feel after weeks of daily marches to reach Saerheim.

He cast occasional glances up at Endyn. Sweat streamed down his brother's huge forehead, and his breath came in labored gasps. Beneath the mask of dirt and road dust, his face was pale with the exertion. He looked one gasp away from collapse.

Fear increased Duvain's burden of weariness. They had left the safety of the Icespire encampment and marched toward the front lines. He'd always known he would fight—he'd signed up for the Legion of Heroes for that very purpose—but now it was all too real. A middling soldier at best, he could march in a straight line most of the time and swing a sword as well as any untrained village boy, but he wasn't cut out for battle. Rear guard or not, they'd been posted too close to the fighting for his comfort.

And that terrified him more than he cared to admit. He wasn't strong like Endyn, fast like Weasel, or a brawler like Rold. He was just a farmer's son armed with standard issue weapons and filled with a nerve-wracking anticipation.

Weasel had spent the entire march south cracking wise, but Owen hadn't spoken a word. He marched with hunched shoulders, back abnormally stiff. Perhaps he, too, felt the fear that dragged on Duvain.

Gritting his teeth against the fire in his legs, spine, and shoulders, he forced himself to match Endyn's pace. He had to stay with his brother, if nothing else. He'd promised as much to his mother before the Bloody Flux claimed her. Endyn needed him as much as he needed Endyn. He gripped his brother's forearm and gave it a reassuring squeeze. Endyn smiled through his pain.

Relief filled him as the sun dipped toward the flat western horizon, and the order to make camp came down the line. He fought the urge to drop his pack and sag to the ground. Instead, he forced himself to keep marching until they reached their designated campsite amid a stand of cedar trees. The moment Sergeant Brash turned away to attend the other platoons under his command, he shrugged out of his pack and sank to the ground with a relieved groan. Endyn did likewise. His face had grown steadily paler throughout the day. He closed his eyes and took deep, ragged breaths.

Weasel looked down at them, a mischievous grin on his face. "Survived the first day, eh?" He snorted.

Behind him, a smile tugged at Owen's lips. "Packs feeling heavy?"

Even Rold's scowl cracked. Grim mirth twinkled in his dark eyes.

Duvain looked between the three men, then at Endyn. He was the butt of some joke, but what?

"Made sure you got all your gear, did you?" Weasel failed to stifle a little laugh. "Got enough to keep you goin' until Dagger Garrison?"

At this, he and Owen burst out laughing, and Rold chuckled.

Duvain's confusion didn't abate. He exchanged a puzzled glance with Endyn. "I…I don't get it."

"Your packs, lads." Corporal Awr's voice drifted over from the patch of grass where he'd taken a seat. "Empty 'em."

Duvain frowned. He'd taken great pains packing his ruck that morning. "Why?"

"Do it," Rold snapped. "That's an order."

After a moment of hesitation, Duvain complied. He spilled the contents of his pack across the ground.

"You, too." Rold said to Endyn, who followed suit.

"Funny thing about fresh meat like you is that they never know what all to pack." Weasel crouched over their piles of stuff. "Yep, as I expected!" He held up the cloth-wrapped bundles Duvain had requested from the camp cook. "They came prepared to feast like kings."

Duvain's forehead wrinkled. "What's wrong with packing a few extra rations?"

"In the grand scheme of things, not a lot." Owen shook his head. "But when you're marching, you want to stick to the bare essentials. Emphasis on *bare*!"

Weasel pawed through Duvain's belongings. "All that armor you're carryin'—helmet, mail shirt, breastplate, gambeson, boots, greaves, bracers, and so on—is goin' to weigh you down. Throw in your shield, short sword, and spear, and the weight adds up." He built a small pile of items off to one side. "There are the things you can't live without: flint for startin' a fire, all-purpose knife, waterskin, and day's rations. A few extras like your wooden bowl and spoon, and you've got enough to weigh you down."

He reached for the three glass jars. "But when you start throwin' in extras, that's when you suffer. The pack gets heavier and heavier with every step, until you end up...well...like this." Weasel's gesture encompassed him and Endyn, sprawled on the ground. "Many an idiot recruit has marched himself into an early grave by packin' too heavy. Though, to be fair, you all handled it a lot better than expected."

Duvain scowled. "And you didn't think to tell us *before* the march?"

Rold shook his head. "No better lesson than experience. You'll make this mistake exactly once." He reached for one of the glass jars. "Stuff like this, this'll slow you—"

Duvain swiped the jar and snatched the other two from Weasel's hands. "There's no way I'm getting rid of these." He stuffed them back into the pack.

"Is that so?" Rold sat up, a cold, spiteful look in his eyes. "And if I ordered you to leave them?"

"I'd take it up with the sergeant, or captain if I had to." Duvain met Rold's gaze without flinching. He'd go to Commander Galerius himself if necessary. The salve in those jars was the only thing keeping Endyn's dragonskin at bay.

Rold snorted and gave a dismissive wave. "Suit yourself. You're the one who'll have to lug it all the way to Dagger Garrison on your back."

A supply wagon rumbled past, depositing one of the collapsible hide tents the Legion used for their marching armies. Owen and Weasel stood and set about erecting the shelter.

39

Rold sneered at them. "Your highnesses, if you'd be so kind as to help?" His face hardened. "Move."

With a groan, Duvain forced himself to his feet. Every muscle from his neck to the soles of his feet ached. His standard-issue boots had rubbed three new blisters into his right foot, with a painful four to match on his left. Each step proved more arduous than the last, but the corporal seemed disinclined to be merciful.

Rold dragged Endyn off to collect firewood from the nearby forest. Duvain had no time to worry for his brother, for Corporal Awr ordered him to lug his fellow Deadheads' packs into the tent. When Rold returned, he set Duvain and Endyn to build the fire, telling them they needed to practice using their flints. Duvain welcomed this last task. He'd had plenty of practice over the freezing winters spent huddling around a tiny fire in the barn. His father had failed to build adequate weatherproofing for their sparse room.

Dinner was a quick production, thanks to the rations he'd hauled from camp. It grated on Duvain to see the others devouring the food he'd packed for himself and Endyn, but kept his complaints to himself. No sense antagonizing the other Deadheads.

"As a reward for a hearty meal," Weasel declared, patting his belly, "let me show you somethin' they don't teach in basic." He produced his wooden spoon and held it up. The handle had been sharpened to a narrow point. "A bit of work, and you've got yourself a skewer to eat with. Handy for those rare occasions when fresh meat's on the menu."

Duvain and Endyn set about sharpening their spoon handles, listening as Owen and Weasel chatted about their journey to Dagger Garrison. They'd be expected to cover at least twenty-five miles per day, but the General could push them up to thirty if the situation on the western front took a turn for the nasty. The thought of covering six hundred miles—fifty times the distance between Northfield and Voramis—filled Duvain with dread.

Owen spent a full half-hour teaching them how to repair their boots. The horsehide exteriors could take a beating, but the woolen interiors would wear out quickly if they got wet. Five layers of laminated

40

leather provided a sturdy sole as well as a bit of cushioning for the feet. Compared to the shoes they'd worn running around Northfield, the boots were a luxury.

Throughout the meal and into the evening, Duvain kept an eye on Endyn. His brother's hand had begun to twitch, his jaw muscles clenching and relaxing. Duvain was worried. The itching had to be driving Endyn mad. When he caught his brother's attention, he held out the jar. Endyn gave a frantic shake of his head.

Duvain understood. His brother was embarrassed by the dragonskin—and why shouldn't he be? It had brought him nothing but ridicule and scorn—but he would rather suffer the torment in silence than show weakness. Weakness had earned them beatings from their father and the other boys in the village.

After a moment, Endyn climbed to his feet and stumbled off into the forest.

"Where's he going?" Rold demanded.

"Nature's calling," Duvain lied.

Rold grunted, but kept his eyes fixed on the forest where Endyn had disappeared.

"Tell me," Duvain asked, trying to divert the corporal's attention, "what are the Fehlans like?"

Rold's head snapped around. "What?"

The ferocity of the corporal's expression surprised Duvain. "The Fehlans. Dagger Garrison's located in their lands, right? I've been wondering why are some of them called Fehlans and some Eirdkilrs?"

Rold snarled. "Do they teach you *nothing* back across the water?"

Duvain met his gaze in silence.

"The name Fehlan literally means 'people of Fehl'. It's a name they gave themselves, but it's like calling us Einari." Rold gestured to each of the men around the fire. "Just like all of us are from different cities—Praamis, Voramis, Malandria, and, in the case of the sergeant,

Drash—the Fehlans have their own clans. Each clan has its own name. For example, the people who once owned the land where Dagger Garrison stands are of the *Deid* clan, or the clan of the Cold Lakes."

"And the Eirdkilrs?" Duvain asked.

Rold continued, "The people we know as Eirdkilrs are actually of the *Tauld* clan, or clan of the Great Wastes, as they call the Wasteland south of the Sawtooth Mountains. When they declared war on us, they changed their name to Eirdkilrs. In the Fehlan tongue, *Eird* means 'half-men'. When you see the size of these savages, you'll understand." He glanced at the forest. "Not quite as big as your brother, but some of them'd give him a run for his money."

"*Eirdkilrs,*" Duvain tried out the name.

"That last part of the name don't need a lot of explainin' does it?" Weasel grinned.

Eirdkilrs. Killers of the half-men. Duvain shuddered.

Weasel's expression grew somber. "No scout's ever made it past the Sawtooth Mountains to find out just how many of them there are livin' in the frozen Wasteland. But we've killed tens of thousands of the bastards since they first showed their ugly faces more than a century ago, yet they still field army after army. They seem to be breedin' new ones as fast as we can cut them down."

The nervousness in Duvain's gut returned. The icy hand of fear gripped the back of his neck.

"But cheer up, meat!" Weasel reached over and slapped his shoulder. "We're safe behind the walls of Dagger Garrison, and there's no way the bastards'll cut through solid stone to reach us. We're as safe as anyone can be in this cold, cruel world." He gave a harsh chuckle.

"Whatever gods you worship, boy," Corporal Awr's rasping voice made the night seem suddenly chill, "get on your knees and pray that's true. Either that, or make your peace with the Long Keeper. When we square off against the Eirdkilrs, you'll be meeting the god of death face to face."

Chapter Four

"Keep up, Deadheads!" Addyn's voice carried toward them as Second Platoon marched past. "Be sure not to stub your toe or get frostbite while the rest of us are doing *real* men's work."

Rold scowled and shot back. "All you'll be doing is finding the enemy's arrows face-first!"

Weasel had a more eloquent response. Duvain's ears burned at the string of profanity spewing from the little man's mouth. Even Endyn seemed shocked.

'That's enough, Private," Rold snapped. "That mouth of yours will get you killed, if you keep running it like that."

"Just givin' our brothers in arms a rousing call to arms," Weasel said, snickering. "Motivatin' them to face the enemy, and all."

Rold shook his head and shouted, "Company, *line!*"

Groaning, Duvain stood from his comfortable seat on the soft grass. When they'd reached the crossroads, the Deadheads had been ordered off the road to allow the rest of the army to pass. Though why, Duvain didn't know. Neither did Owen, Weasel, or any of the others, apparently.

As soon as the last of the Legionnaires marched past, Sergeant Brash and the other four squad sergeants barked orders to hurry the men.

Duvain glanced at Captain Lingram. The captain sat on his horse at the head of the line, his expression somber as he studied his company.

Beside him, Endyn shuffled in place. The twitch in his hand had gotten bad, and he'd begun muttering to himself, the way he always did when the itching grew unbearable. Weeks of marching in the heavy armor had to have made the dragonskin uncomfortable. He'd be going mad, but unable to do anything about it without breaking formation— and suffering terrible punishments at the hand of Rold, Brash, and the other officers. Worse, the supply of unguent was nearly exhausted.

"The minute we break camp tonight," Duvain told his brother in a low voice, "we'll get some of that salve on it."

Endyn met his gaze, and misery filled his expression. The itch was just one of the dragonskin's effects—the thick scales would chap and crack, causing the skin around them to grow red, raw, and painful.

Duvain felt sorry for his brother, but he could only grip Endyn's massive forearm and squeeze. "You've got this," he whispered. "Just a little longer."

"Any idea what this is about?" Owen whispered to Weasel.

"Not a bleedin' clue." Weasel shrugged. "But the Captain'll tell us what we need to know when he figgers we need to know it."

Captain Lingram remained silent, as if waiting for the last dust of the departing Legionnaires to settle and leave the Deadheads alone on the Westmarch. Duvain's nerves grew more ragged with every quiet minute. Something told him a change in the aforementioned plans to march to Dagger Garrison was coming. A change he *wouldn't* like.

His eyes scanned the thick woods bordering the Legion-built stone highway. After living among the plains of southern Einan, the terrain around Duvain had an almost magical beauty. Dense forests of oak, pine, elm, and aspen trees stretched in all directions, a sea of greens, browns, and reds that glowed in the bright sunlight. To the west, steep hills rose to vertical rocky cliffs of a brilliant white. To the east, the colors of nature deepened, marking the presence of bogs, marshes, and swamplands. His gaze drifted south, as if expecting to see the jagged ridges of the Sawtooth Mountains far beyond the horizon. His mind filled with images of the mystical creatures—frost bears, white mountain apes, even the fabled ice dragons—that were said to occupy the icy Wastelands beyond.

The Eirdkilrs lived there as well. He'd heard tales of the huge, shaggy-haired men of the Wastelands. Tales that sent a shiver down his spine as surely as the chill of the ice floes of the Frozen Sea. The thought of facing them in battle set his hands quivering.

"We've just received new orders from Commander Galerius." Captain Lingram's voice snapped Duvain back to attention. "We are to march to Saerheim, where we'll take up residence among the Deid and provide support for our Fehlan allies. We may not be fighting the Eirdkilrs directly, men, but our duty is no less important. As much an honor as meeting the enemy head on."

Rold gave a quiet snort beside Duvain. "Honor, my hairy arse."

The captain turned to Sergeant Awr. "We move out at once. Saerheim is two days and a half of fast-march, so we've no time to waste." Despite his calm expression, his tone held a hint of urgency Duvain didn't understand. "Move out!"

At the shouted order, the line of Legionnaires broke into a march, heading south in pursuit of their departing comrades.

"Hah!" Weasel laughed softly. "Y'hear that, lads? For once, the gods show us their smiles instead of their puckered arseholes!" He hitched up his chain mail shirt and scratched vigorously at his rear. "Marchin'll be rough through all that dense forest and those awful roads—little more than muddy beaten paths, really. But once we reach Saerheim, we've got the cushy job. Providin' support means sittin' around that Fehlan village, eatin', drinkin', standin' watch. All very humdrum and dull." He turned now and grinned at Duvain. "Just the way I like it."

Owen shook his head. "Just remember, no adding to your ear collection while in Saerheim. They're all friendly Fehlans, allied with the Princelands and aiding us in our war efforts against the Eirdkilrs."

Weasel muttered something that sounded like "can't tell the Keeper-damned savages apart".

Duvain cast a worried glance at Endyn. His brother needed rest to give his dragonskin time to heal and the unguent to soothe the pain.

At the crossroads, Captain Lingram led the way east, down a road as bad as Weasel had described. Calling the muddy, winding track through the forest a "road" was far too generous. Yet Duvain welcomed the change in direction and posting. He gave silent thanks to the Swordsman, god of war, that they would be stationed far from the front. Someplace safe and quiet, like a little Fehlan village in the middle of nowhere. After the stories he'd heard of the Eirdkilrs over the last weeks of marching—stories vastly different from the tales of glory and heroism told by Legion recruiters in Voramis—he had no desire to face the enemy head-on.

Especially not with the men surrounding him. The Deadheads numbered fewer than one hundred and twenty, including Captain Lingram. More than a few had paunches far thicker than Legion regulation permitted. Some sported wounds just shy of debilitating. Only a few bore the professional demeanor of true Legionnaires—according to Owen, all of those had followed Captain Lingram to the Deadheads after his demotion. Corporal Awr was one of those, as was Sergeant Brash and another of the sergeants.

In the next row, Weasel was shaking his head. "This ain't good. The company couldn't hold off a stiff breeze."

A week earlier, Weasel had estimated Ninth Company could field twenty men capable of proper battle. The rest—and Weasel included Duvain and Endyn among that number—would do little more than serve as meat shields and arrow magnets.

But we're not going to fight, he told himself. *We're just going to guard a village far from the front.*

Yet, try as he might, he couldn't shake the doubt that nagged at the back of his mind.

* * *

"Four more hours!" Weasel crowed. "Four more hours until we put up our feet and enjoy the easy life!"

After two cold nights in the forest and the better part of three days spent marching down the muddy wagon road, Duvain was more than ready to buy into Weasel's idea of their new assignment. His feet, legs, and back definitely wanted him either to hurry or not to move at all. His shoulders felt like they'd forever bear the indents of his rucksack. Even though he'd emptied out all the unnecessary items, it still weighed too much. The wooden frame rubbed his back and hips raw. His blisters had worsened with each new day, though thankfully no new ones had formed after Owen instructed him to double up on his woolen socks.

None of the others seemed to mind the march—no more so than usual, at least. Legionnaires tended to grumble about everything: from the occasional rain to the bloody heat to the blistering, Keeper-damned cold nights to the piss-poor chow. Weasel, in particular, found something new to complain about every hour.

As if on cue, Weasel took up a rant about the ugly backside of the Legionnaire marching in front of him. The man ignored him as Weasel spouted nonsense about his womanly shoulders, bullish hips, and flat arse. By the time he got to "chicken legs", Owen had had enough.

"Shut up, Weasel!" he snapped. "Can you just keep your mouth shut for a Watcher-damned minute? I'd rather listen to Endyn's snoring than your constant whingeing."

Endyn colored. The previous night, in a moment of irritation, Rold had described Endyn's snoring as "a cross between a constipated horse fart and the braying of a drunk donkey". None of the other Deadheads appeared to care that Endyn could do nothing about the problem, another side effect of whatever caused him to grow to his massive size.

Weasel remained unfazed by Owen's outburst. "Talkin' helps to pass the time. Not all of us believe in the righteousness of our cause like you do." Disdain echoed in his voice.

"Of course," Owen snarled. "It's all about the gold with you!"

"Why shouldn't it be?" Weasel asked. "Most of us are only here because it's the best way to earn a livin'. When you're good at somethin', you find a way to use that skill to turn a coin. Just so happens most of us are pretty darned good at killin'."

Owen snorted. "How noble of you."

"Nobility is for the pompous lords and ladies." Weasel's shrug jostled his pack. "Some of us don't have the luxury of nobility. Either we join the Legion, get drafted into a gang, or swing at the end of a hangman's noose. I know which I choose. Besides," he gestured to the forest around him, "I get the chance to see the world. Before I joined, I never thought I'd get out of Lower Voramis, much less the city. Now, I've seen more of the world than I ever expected. I don't mind dyin' away from the piss-hole I was raised in. Not all of us have somethin' to return home to."

Duvain found himself nodding. He and Endyn had joined because Northfield had no longer felt like home after the death of their parents. Everywhere he looked, he saw the pain of his childhood, his life under his father's boot, watching Endyn suffer for his condition. The Legion had given him a way out, both him and Endyn. And a hope for a future. The coins they'd earn serving here would go a long way toward setting up a life. What he'd do after his service, he didn't know, but it was enough that he'd have options—something he never had in Northfield.

He allowed himself the luxury of daydreaming. Images of what his future could hold distracted him from the drudgery of marching. It took little effort to keep in step with Weasel's back, and the rest of his attention could go toward imagining a bright, hopeful future.

As they marched, the woods grew denser, thickening in a way only old-growth forests could. The muddy track wound through the towering trees, and it seemed the yew, elm, and oak branches reached toward them, welcoming them with leafy boughs. The pine and aspen trees grew straight and tall, reaching conceited heads high into the sky. A cool wind whispered all around them, turning the shade of the forest decidedly chilly.

Around a bend in the road, they came upon a patch of open, muddy ground that spread out a few hundred paces from the west side of the road. Fallen trees and dead logs littered the space. The track curved around the expanse. As the column passed the open space, a sound filtered into Duvain's ears. Almost like someone was cutting wood, similar to the sounds he'd heard back at the lumber camp outside Northfield.

He glanced around, nervous. Maybe the Fehlan were working nearby?

"Woodcutters!" the shout came from two rows back. Real fear echoed in the cry.

He jerked around, scanning the forest for any sign of attack. He had no idea why woodcutters would be a source of concern, but this close to the front, he wouldn't take chances.

His eyes darted through the trees, but no barbarians charged from the woods, no war cries broke the silence. Instead, a flicker of movement on the ground caught his attention.

A serpent darted from beneath a fallen log. Though not large— barely the length of Duvain's forearm—it had bulging eyes, shielded nostrils, and a short, rounded snout. It slithered in an odd sidewinding undulation, and the movement set its emerald green and bone white scales rubbing against each other with a buzzing sound like a steel saw biting into a thick tree trunk.

The man behind Duvain cried out and leapt back. Endyn never saw the viper before it buried its fangs in his leg. His eyes went wide in fear, and he froze as the snake's jaws clamped tight on his calf. Rold reacted before either of them—he drew his short sword and chopped off the serpent's head in one stroke. The body twitched and writhed, flopping around.

"Back!" Rold shouted. He seized Endyn by the collar and dragged him away from the muddy expanse. Even as he did, two more of the green, scaled vipers reared up from the ground. They coiled like a figure eight, head poised in the center, ready to lash out at the nearest Legionnaire. All the while, their scales made the terrifying whirring sound.

Weasel's dagger took one in the head, pinning it to the sand. The other darted toward the column of marching men, only to be met by the metal rim of a Legionnaire's shield.

The sawing sound grew louder for a moment, then slowly quietened.

"Damn it!" Rold cursed. "A Keeper-damned woodcutter viper pit." His finger indicated the patch of fallen logs a short distance from the road. "Deadheads, keep well away from there if you don't want to end up dead like this one."

Endyn's eyes went wide. "Dead?" he rumbled.

Weasel's face was pale. "Woodcutters are high on the list of don't-fuck-with snakes. Little bastards burrow into the sand and sleep the day away. They're bloody feisty if pissed off. And the venom's enough to kill a grown man twenty times over. Anyone who gets bit…" He trailed off, his eyes darting away. "Sorry, Endyn."

Rold was kneeling, his knife already out and sawing at Endyn's pants. Cloth tore, and the corporal scanned Endyn's leg.

"Bloody Minstrel!" he recoiled, nearly falling onto his ass. "What in the frozen hell is *that*?"

Weasel gasped at the sight of Endyn's leg, and Owen's face had gone a strange green. Duvain's heart sank. He recognized the patches of scaled skin, the red cracks covering Endyn's shin and calf to the ankle. The dragonskin had spread. It was worse than he expected.

"Whatever it is," Rold said, his voice a mixture of revulsion and incredulity, "it just saved your life."

The words took a moment to sink in. "What?" Duvain asked.

"A woodcutter's bite packs enough venom to take down a full squad of men, and then some." Rold tapped the tip of his dagger on the thick scale. "But this shite's so thick the serpent's fangs couldn't get through." He ripped the bottom of Endyn's pants and used the fabric to wipe a stream of clear liquid dribbling down his leg. He held it up to them. "See this? The bastard sprayed his load all over, but his fangs never punctured the skin."

Face burning with embarrassment, Endyn quickly tugged the pant leg down over the dragonskin.

Duvain extended a hand to help Endyn up, and Rold did the same. The corporal stared up at Endyn through narrowed eyes. "Does the captain know about…" He gestured to Endyn's leg. "…that?"

Endyn glanced at Duvain, who shook his head. "No, and he doesn't need to know."

Rold raised an eyebrow. "Is that so?"

Duvain met Rold's, Weasel's, and Owen's eyes in turn. "It won't spread, if that's what you're worried about."

The three Deadheads exchanged suspicious looks.

"Look," Duvain insisted, "it's something he's had since he was young, but it can't be passed on. The healers at the Sanctuary said as much."

After a long moment, Rold shook his head. "Captain still needs to know."

"It's his way of things." Awr's quiet rasping voice cut in.

Duvain's head flashed around.

Awr had come up without a sound. He stood behind Weasel, staring at Endyn, yet without disdain or disgust on his face. "He cares about his men. He's unlike most commanders that way."

Duvain met Awr's gaze. He could have stared at stone. The man was hard, not cold, but revealing as much as the stone cliffs to the west. "Very well. But I'll tell him."

Rold scowled. "Chain of command says—"

"*I* will tell him." Duvain clenched his fists.

After a moment, Rold snorted and shrugged. "You have until end of day."

Duvain's gut clenched, but he nodded. "So be it."

Rold held his glance for a long moment. The look had as much warmth as if the corporal were staring at a rake or a feather duster. Rold didn't care about him—all that mattered was that his comrades wouldn't get him killed in battle.

The tension snapped, and Rold turned to the rest of the company. "What are you lot doing, sitting about like doxies on holiday? Back in line!" he roared.

The rest of the Deadheads hurried to form up. A low mutter ran through the ranks. Duvain hoped none of them had seen Endyn's leg, but there was no mistaking the hushed whispers, the backward glances. They'd seen the woodcutter viper bite Endyn, yet Corporal Rold was treating everything like business as usual. That spawned speculation aplenty.

The sound of hoofbeats grew louder. Duvain looked up to see Captain Lingram trotting down the line of men toward them.

"All is well, Corporal?" he asked Awr.

"Aye, Captain." Awr nodded.

Rold interjected. "Spot of bother with a nest of woodcutter vipers." He shot Duvain a look. "Got it sorted out."

"Good." Captain Lingram nodded. "We've a good deal of ground to cover, and Skelan tells me our path leads through some heavy woods that'll get dark before the sun sets."

"Aye, sir!" Corporal Rold saluted.

With a nod, Captain Lingram turned his horse and rode toward the front of the line. A moment later, Sergeant Brash's barked orders of "Company, march!" echoed out.

Duvain's eyes widened when Weasel darted out of rank to snatch up the decapitated serpent's body.

Weasel shot him a grin. "Just because they bite like bastards, don't mean they taste like 'em. No sense wastin' good meat, says I—anythin' is better than rations."

Owen shook his head.

"What?" Weasel protested. "It's not like I'm riskin' *my* hide huntin' them down. Thanks to Endyn here," he winked up at the big man, "we've got ourselves a little somethin' extra for supper tonight. Gods alone know what sort of grub they'll serve at the Fehlan village."

He pointed to the muddy patch of ground and the pile of fallen logs. "You see anythin' like that in these parts, you steer bloody well clear. Even you, big man. That's where they hang out, and I doubt even *you* can survive for long."

Endyn nodded. "Got it."

Duvain noticed that Endyn seemed subdued, shy. He looked at the men around him with wary eyes. The other Deadheads also shot him occasional glances, and a gap had opened around their rank. Sorrow weighed on Duvain, but the reaction came as no surprise. People tended to act like that when they saw Endyn's dragonskin—it was why he kept it hidden.

Tension lined his brother's face. His jaw muscles worked, and as the hours of marching wore on, the twitching in his hand grew more pronounced. Once, he actually reached up and scratched at his neck. Duvain caught a hint of grey above his collar and cursed. He had to get some of the salve on Endyn's dragonskin before it spread. The fatigue of the march and the emotional turmoil hiding behind Endyn's stony expression would only make things worse.

From a young age, Endyn had been his mother's favorite, and the arrival of Duvain a few years later did little to change that. Even after he reached his gigantic height, his mother had been gentle, tender with him. Endyn was a gentle soul, one who wanted to be liked and accepted by everyone. His size made him stand out, so he tried to work extra hard to fit in.

The dragonskin was a curse, one that kept others at bay. The previous day, when the Deadheads found a stream to wash in, Endyn

53

had refused to undress with the others. He'd sat on the bank and watched as Owen, Weasel, Rold, and the other Deadheads relaxed in the cool water. Their cramped tent offered no privacy for him to change, so he would disappear into the woods to scratch the itch away from the eyes of his comrades. But now they knew his shameful secret, and their sidelong glances pained him.

Duvain hated to see his brother suffer so—physically and emotionally. Though Endyn was the older brother, Duvain had always looked out for him. He'd continue to do so, even if it meant being the one to face Captain Lingram's wrath when he told him Endyn's secret.

His mood soured as the forest grew denser. The thick canopy blocked out the sunlight, and a chill wind whispered through the woods. The shadows hung heavy about them as they marched through the eerie silence.

"Bloody trees," Weasel muttered. "You can't trust 'em."

"Think they'll uproot themselves and bite you?" Owen teased.

Weasel glared. "'Course not, because I ain't an idiot." He punched Owen's shoulder. "But you never know what's hidin' in trees that thick."

The image of a pack of shrieking barbarians ran through Duvain's mind. He'd never seen an Eirdkilr before, but had heard the descriptions: howling savages clad in furs, waving huge weapons, shaking the ground with their war cries. He gripped his shield tighter. With every step, the forests grew more impenetrable, the shadows deepening. Fear thrummed in the back of his mind; his imagination screamed that the densely packed trees concealed an army of Eirdkilrs come to massacre them all.

He nearly cried in relief as the thick forest gave way to a clearing. The muddy track cut straight across the open ground, climbing a short incline toward a palisade wall. The tension drained from his shoulders. They had reached Saerheim.

The walls around Saerheim, erected by a Legionnaire company stationed there years earlier, stood roughly three paces tall. Once, the sharpened stakes would have deterred enemies from climbing over; time and weather had dulled the keen points. But the wall stretched a full three hundred paces across, with a heavy gate in the center.

54

Beyond the wall, Duvain caught a glimpse of a cliff's edge, with farmland spreading out below. In the distance, a few hundred paces from the cliff, the turquoise water of Cold Lake sparkled in the fading sunlight.

The gates swung open at their approach.

"Company, HALT!" Sergeant Brash shouted. The column of Legionnaires stopped just short of the opening gate.

The man who emerged to greet them had to be closing in on his seventh decade. He wore thick woolen breeches, a sheepskin vest over a simple tunic, and a cloak of heavy fur. His eyes and mouth were lined by sun and mirth, but he walked with a straight back. He smiled and spread his arms. "Greetings, men of Icespire." He spoke Einari with a thick accent.

Captain Lingram dismounted and strode toward the man. "Elder Asmund of Saerheim, I am Captain Lingram of the Ninth Company. You do us honor with your greeting." He continued speaking, but in a language Duvain didn't recognize.

The elder's eyes lit up. "You speak our tongue?" he asked in Einari.

"Not well, I fear." Captain Lingram replied. "The people of the *Fjall* clan would be ashamed to hear me, believing their lessons wasted."

Duvain's eyebrows rose. The *Fjall* were the largest and most powerful of the clans north of the Sawtooth Mountains. Captain Lingram had spent time among them?

"Few of your kind have tried to learn, so it is a welcome change." He stepped aside and swept an arm toward the open gate. "I welcome you to Saerheim. We have prepared a place for your men to stay while you are here."

"We have our own tents, and—"

Elder Asmund shook his head. "The *Saer* is a cold place at night. Your tents will do little to keep out the cold rolling off the lake. Our structures may be simple, but they are warm."

Captain Lingram bowed. "You do us honor, Elder Asmund."

"It is no more than our peace accords demands." The old man's weathered face broke into a smile. "Now, come, enter Saerheim and find rest."

At the captain's command, the Legionnaires marched into the village.

Duvain couldn't help staring at everything around him. People dressed in simple garb like Elder Asmund's stared at them as they entered. Women carried baskets of wool, tended cook fires, or hustled after energetic children. The few men they encountered busied themselves applying a fresh layer of daub to the wattle walls of their simple wooden homes.

The road led from the gate, past a collection of small, single-room houses, toward a broad expanse of paved stone—no doubt Saerheim's main square. Four huge longhouses faced the main square, stretching easily seven or eight paces wide, five paces tall, and at least twenty paces long. These structures were made of sturdy logs, their roofs covered with thick layers of thatching to keep out the chill.

When the Legionnaires reached the paved stone square, Sergeant Brash called for a halt.

Endyn gave an audible groan. Duvain glanced up at him. Tears brimmed in his brother's eyes, and he shifted from foot to foot in visible discomfort. He breathed through his massive nostrils, as if struggling to restrain himself. The pain had to be bad.

Sergeant Brash strode toward them. "Squad Three, get settled into your billets, get some chow, and prepare for midnight watch."

Corporal Rold snapped a salute. "Yes, Sergeant."

Sergeant Brash moved on to the next squad, giving orders in his calm, even voice.

"You heard him, lads!" Weasel turned with a grin. "Midnight's still a ways off. I wonder what sort of trouble we can get into before then."

"None," Corporal Rold barked. "We're doing exactly as the sergeant says. We stay in quarters until it's time for watch." He stabbed a finger at Weasel's chest. "And lose the jewelry."

Weasel glanced down at his grisly necklace. "Aww, really, Corporal?"

Rold snarled. "Now, soldier!" He glanced around. "No need to antagonize the natives further."

Duvain eyed the villagers of Saerheim. The Fehlan watched them with hooded, studied expressions, turning away whenever he looked at them. None spoke or approached. Though they showed no overt hatred, a tense silence hung in the air. They were *not* welcome guests.

Grumbling, Weasel removed his necklace of ears and tucked it into his shirt.

A middle-aged man with a straw-colored beard strode toward them, speaking in Fehlan. Surprisingly, Corporal Awr responded in the same tongue. The villager raised an eyebrow and tried to engage in conversation with Awr, but the corporal only shrugged. After a moment, the man gave up and gestured for them to follow him.

The Fehlan villager led them to the northwest side of the village, toward a house that stood just a short distance from the main square. It was small, just five paces wide and six long, with a roof barely higher than Endyn's head. Thick mud had been caked over the woven sticks as weatherproofing. The man said something in Fehlan and motioned toward the house.

With a nod for the bearded villager, Awr turned to the rest of them. "This is us." He strode toward the open door and entered.

The interior was small, far smaller than Duvain had expected. Three wooden steps descended to a single room dug below the level of the ground outside. The people of Saerheim lived simply. The room had no windows or any decorations—only a door and a space to live.

"Damn!" Weasel muttered. "Looks like we're goin' to be nut to butt in here."

"When the nights get cold," Corporal Awr replied, "you'll be glad for your comrade's body heat."

Weasel turned to glare at them. "Just make sure none of you go pokin' anythin' into me when I sleep, eh?"

Duvain rolled his eyes and entered the hovel. He selected a corner of the room and dumped his pack there, making space for Endyn beside him.

Weasel muttered. "Damn, with the big man here, we're goin' to be even tighter. It'll be like—"

With a rumbling sob, Endyn shoved past Weasel and rushed toward his pack. He nearly ripped the drawstrings open with his frantic pawing.

Duvain's eyes widened. He'd never seen it this bad before.

"What in the bloody hell?" Weasel asked, picking himself up from the ground. "What's gotten into him?"

Ignoring the others, Duvain rushed toward Endyn. "Ditch the armor, I'll get the salve."

Endyn's eyes shot toward the men crowded at the door, but after a moment of hesitation, began ripping at his armor.

Duvain heard the *clink* of the breastplate falling, followed by the jingling of his mail shirt. By the time he'd dug the jar from his pack, Endyn was out of his gambeson and down to his undertunic, which he pulled over his head with frantic movements.

Duvain gasped at the sight of Endyn's back. The thick, grey scales had grown to the thickness of his finger, the cracks running between them turned an angry red. Sweat and dirt clung to the weeping sores. Pus dribbled from a fresh wound in his side. Endyn scratched at himself frantically, his huge fingers nearly ripping the scaly flesh in his desperation to stifle the itching.

"Endyn, stop!" Duvain shouted. "That'll only make it worse."

Endyn was beyond caring. Tears streamed down his face, and sobs of misery set his shoulders heaving. The dragonskin was worsening at a far faster rate than Duvain had dreamed.

He whirled on the others. "Help me hold his arms!"

Owen, Weasel, and Corporal Rold stood open-mouthed, gaping at the sight of Endyn squirming and pawing at his encrusted flesh.

"Help me!" Duvain shouted again.

Corporal Rold reacted first, seizing Endyn's right arm and tugging it out to the side. Endyn cried out and tried to break free, but Owen and Weasel seized his other arm.

"Get him on the ground!" Duvain shouted. "If he scratches too hard, he'll tear the scales wide open."

The four of them wrestled Endyn flat onto his stomach, no easy task given Endyn's enormous size and strength. The huge man protested, tears streaming. Duvain wept at his brother's misery, but he had no choice. He had to stop Endyn from making the problem worse.

"Whatever you're going to do," Rold shouted, "better get on with it!"

Duvain fumbled the jar lid open and scooped a handful of the cream from within. He slathered it over Endyn's back, coating the scales and the raw, weeping skin with a thick layer. Slowly, Endyn's struggles quieted, and he lay still. Owen, Weasel, and Corporal Rold clung to his arms, breathing heavily.

When Duvain had covered his back, he nodded to them. "You can release him."

The three Legionnaires leapt back as if afraid of getting burned. Rold wiped his palms on his uniform, and Owen simply stared down at his hands, as if expecting to see grey scales form.

Duvain ignored them. He helped Endyn to sit up, and he applied another layer of the salve to his brother's chest. Endyn sobbed, but the cries were more from relief than of pain. He closed his eyes and leaned his head against the hut wall.

The smell of the salve filled the hut. The jar was nearly empty by the time Duvain had covered Endyn's enormous chest and torso. He carefully replaced the lid and tucked the jar into his pack, letting out a long, slow breath. He turned to his brother, who gave him a grateful nod. The flow of tears had slowed but not stopped. Though cream soothed the itch and dimmed the burning pain, it didn't alleviate the torment completely.

Even seated, Endyn was nearly as tall as Duvain was standing. Duvain gripped the back of Endyn's neck and leaned his forehead against his brother's. He could find no words, but simply remained there, sharing his brother's suffering in the only way he knew how.

The only sound to break the silence came from the wooden door closing behind his departing comrades.

Chapter Five

"And you're *certain* this won't affect anyone else?"

Duvain cringed under Captain Lingram's stare. There was no recrimination in the captain's eyes, only concern. He nodded. "No, sir. The healers at the Sanctuary in Voramis spent weeks poking and prodding him, and though they didn't find any solution, they determined it's not contagious." He rolled up his sleeves to reveal his unblemished arms. "I've been touching it for years and not a thing."

Captain Lingram pondered a moment, then nodded. "Then we've no problems." He tapped the hilt of his sword with a long fingernail. "You say the itch gets bad after a few hours in armor?"

Duvain nodded. "Yes, sir."

"Nothing to be done about that, but I'll let Sergeant Brash know your brother may need to take the occasional break to have a moment to himself. Should make it a bit more bearable."

Duvain's eyes widened. "Thank you, Captain!" He'd expected recrimination and vitriol, and the captain's reaction caught him off guard. No one had treated Endyn with such understanding, even compassion.

Captain Lingram gripped Duvain's shoulder. "Man like him, he's the sort who will come in handy if we ever find ourselves in trouble. I've seen commanders use up their men like a wastrel spending gold, and that never turns out well. If Garrow's Canyon taught me one thing, it's *always* take care of your assets. I'd have died there if not for a one-armed soldier who threw himself in the path of an enemy axe. Lost his other arm, but walked away from that battle alive. One of the few who did. A man's outward appearance or lack of skill *never* dictates his true limitations. Remember that for when you rise in the ranks."

"I will, sir!"

"Good." Captain Lingram nodded. "Now, I believe Squad Three has the midnight watch."

Duvain snapped a crisp salute. "Aye, Captain!" He turned and marched toward the hut where he and his squad bunked. He understood why Awr and the others had followed Captain Lingram to the Deadheads. He, too, had seen officers who pushed their men to breaking and discarded them when they no longer served a purpose. Captain Lingram was the sort of officer worth following, it seemed.

A shadow passed over Endyn's face as Duvain entered their hut, and his brow furrowed.

"Don't worry, Brother." Duvain gave him a small smile. "Captain says you're good."

The relief in Endyn's eyes mirrored Duvain's own. "Thank you," he rumbled.

Duvain smiled at his brother. "Let's get you into your armor. We've got a watch to stand."

* * *

Duvain's gut clenched as they approached the brazier burning beside the southeast corner of Saerheim. Owen and Weasel sat next to the fire, warming their hands against the chill that had descended on the village after dark. They glanced up at him and Endyn, then quickly looked away.

The two of them and Rold had acted strange since that afternoon—exactly what Endyn feared. They looked at him with new eyes, as if staring at a freak in the Praamian circus. Beyond the basics of their watch, none of them had spoken since the shift began.

Duvain glanced at Endyn. The pain in his brother's eyes didn't come from the dragonskin—the salve would soothe the itching and pain until morning. No, the pain came from the harsh truth: no matter where he went, he would always be an outcast. He had been since a young age, thanks to his height. The dragonskin just compounded the problem.

With a sigh, Duvain turned his back on the fire and took another lap of their patrol.

Rold had paired the two of them together, assigning them a patrol of Saerheim's west side. They'd entered through the western gate earlier that day, and not even animals moved across the empty expanse of ground between the village and the forest. They were essentially guarding the village's rear, certainly a punishment of some sort. With the front line far to the southeast, there was more chance of their wall being overrun by the woodcutter vipers than by Eirdkilrs.

Duvain found himself wishing for a patrol along the eastern wall. The wall ran parallel to the edge of the cliff atop which Saerheim sat, and was really the only direction from which a threat could come. Here in Saerheim, far from the front, there would be no risk of an Eirdkilr attack. He wanted to use the few quiet moments, those not spent in ceaseless patrol, to look out over Cold Lake to the southwest. It reminded him of Hunter's Lake outside of Northfield, the place where he and Endyn had spent many happy hours laughing, splashing, and swimming as boys. The lake's mirror surface reflected the moonlight, and the stars glimmered like a thousand sparkling jewels. In the morning, tendrils of mist would creep onto the land like ghosts of legend come to visit the land of the living.

Sighing, he turned his attention back to his patrol. Saerheim was smaller than he'd expected. Roughly three hundred Fehlans made their home here. Most lived in the four massive longhouses fronting the village's main square. The village's only blacksmith had a large house and attached smithy on the southwest corner. Beside him, the weaver, potter, and wheelwright plied their trades in smaller houses. A few families chose to live in their own small houses, made of wattle and daub with thatched roofs barely able to keep out the winter chill.

Back when Weasel had been on speaking terms with them, he'd gone on about how towns and villages among the Fehlan were distinguished by the purpose of the settlement. Villages existed to farm, herd sheep and cattle, and make the goods they needed to live. Towns did all that, but they also provided a hub for traders to buy and sell goods, thriving on the presence of trade rather than the consumption of their own produce.

The main square was fifty paces on all sides, with a well on the southeastern corner and dominated by a broad courtyard paved with dark grey bluestone. It was here that the people of the village would gather, Weasel said, for their celebrations, festivals, and whatever other "savage" rituals they engaged in. The people here lived simple lives: farmers, shepherds, and woodcutters content to scratch out a comfortable existence from the land. Why they had been sent here was beyond Duvain.

The palisade wall was certainly not of the villagers' doing. According to Owen, a garrison of Legionnaires had erected the structure during the conquest of Fehl a century before.

The Legionnaires had chosen a good site for their fort. Saerheim had been built near enough to the lake for the villagers to have easy access to fresh water, but the village itself sat upon a high cliff. Their position provided excellent visibility of the surrounding area to spot any unwelcome visitors. A single muddy road—wide enough for a horse- or ox-drawn cart to navigate—descended from the eastern gate to the farmlands below. Channels had been cut into the earth to supply the land with water for crops. Aside from the food grown on the farms, the villagers hunted in the woods and caught fish in Cold Lake. Yet, should they find themselves in peril, they could retreat behind the palisade wall and close the gates. A company of Legionnaires could hold off two or three times their number.

Duvain found himself fascinated by the Fehlans. He'd expected fur-clad savages in war paint, as the tales of the Eirdkilr War suggested, but the people here resembled villagers on Einan. They wore tunics and breeches, made from wool and cut in a simple style. The colors, however, were brighter than even the popular cloth in Voramis. The blues, especially, were deep and rich. The product of the glastum plant, he'd heard.

The problem was that none of the Fehlans seemed inclined to talk. If any of the people in the village spoke even basic Einari, they hadn't made an attempt to open dialogue. Indeed, the few they'd encountered that afternoon had quickly scurried the other way when they tried to talk. One had even shot them a venomous glare before striding in the opposite direction.

He contemplated the villagers' dislike of them. Weren't they here to *protect* Saerheim? Why would the people hate them?

When they reached the end of their next round, they found the brazier abandoned by all but Corporal Awr. Weasel, Owen, and Rold were walking the wooden rampart platforms on the interior of the wall. The grizzled corporal sat alone, his back to the fire, staring off into the night.

"Corporal, you were speaking Fehlan earlier, right?" Duvain asked.

Corporal Awr gave him a sharp look, but said nothing.

"Can you teach me some?"

Awr's look changed to one of mild surprise. "Why?"

Duvain shrugged. "I figure if we're going to be here a while, it could come in handy, knowing a few words."

For a long moment, Awr fixed him with a piercing glare, then shook his head. "Don't waste your time."

It was Duvain's turn to be surprised. "What?"

Awr spoke without meeting Duvain's gaze. "It won't do anything. They aren't going to like you, any way you cut it. After all, we've kicked them out of their homes."

Duvain's eyes widened. He hadn't given it much thought. The village had a few small houses, no doubt each built for a family. If they occupied one of the homes, it meant one of the families had to be evicted. With all one hundred-twenty men of Ninth Company, that meant a lot of displaced villagers, no doubt crammed into the longhouses.

Awr stood. "Listen, meat, we're here because we have to be, but none of us *want* to be—not us, and certainly not the Fehlan. All they want is to be left alone to tend to their farms, cattle, and fish. They'd rather have nothing to do with the war—they'd be perfectly happy if they never saw an Eirdkilr, Princelander, or Einari face. But we've brought that war to them, and they're doing what they do best: surviving. But that doesn't mean they have to like it, or us."

Duvain swallowed. Awr spoke infrequently—he'd barely said a word over four days of marching, except in response to Captain Lingram or Sergeant Brash's orders—but when he did, he delivered piercing insight.

"Still," Duvain said, hesitant, "I'd still like to learn a bit of the Fehlan tongue."

Awr said nothing for a long moment. Silence stretched on, broken only by the crack of the firewood and the churring trill of a nightjar. Finally, Awr shrugged. "Fine. Not like we've a whole lot better to do around here."

Duvain smiled. "Thank you."

"It'll cost you, though." Awr growled. "Bring me something to drink—wine, ale, or whatever swill is brewed here—and I'll teach you."

Duvain's smile faded. He had no idea where to find liquor. Without his first pay from the Legion, he had no coins to buy with. He'd have to find another way. But how?

A solution presented itself at the end of their watch. One of Squad Four's privates stumbled from his bed mumbling about a hangover. When Duvain offered to take his watch in exchange for the liquor he'd imbibed too much of, the man gladly agreed to the trade.

Worry lined Endyn's face. He looked tired—the hours of endless walking had taken its toll on him.

"Go," Duvain told him. "Rest."

Endyn raised a questioning eyebrow.

"I'll be fine. I couldn't sleep anyway." A yawn forced itself past Duvain's lips.

Endyn snorted.

"Look, I *have* to do this." Duvain dropped his voice. "You've seen the way the others look at us. *Both* of us."

Endyn's face clouded, and pain filled his eyes.

"If doing this will earn me a bit of goodwill with the other squads and Corporal Awr, you know I'm going to." Duvain stifled another yawn without success. "I'll find time to sleep before next watch." The Legion divided their days between rest, drilling and training, and standing guard. He had just volunteered his rest time—he'd be in for a long session of marching, weapons practice, and formation drills. But he'd get through it.

Endyn hesitated, but Duvain shoved him away. "Off with you." His stomach gave a growl nearly as loud as Endyn's snores. "But bring me some chow, will you?"

Nodding, Endyn lumbered away from the watch post. When he disappeared, Duvain groaned and sagged to a seat in front of the dying fire. His feet and back ached, and his armor felt as if it weighed far too much. He wanted nothing more than to rest. Sadly, he wouldn't have a chance to—

"Riders, in the east!" The shout from behind him snapped him from his gloom. Immediately, he was on full alert, his heart racing and adrenaline pumping. A sudden fear raced through him. Were they under attack?

Danver, the Fourth Squad sergeant, rushed past him. "On your feet, Legionnaire!"

Duvain realized he hadn't moved. Panic had rooted him in place. His stomach churned, and he felt as if he'd vomit. He was afraid, and hated himself for it.

The sight of Captain Lingram striding toward the eastern gate galvanized him into action. He stood and rushed after the sergeant, taking his place on the wooden ramparts beside the rest of Squad Four.

He caught a flash of white through the early morning mist rolling off Cold Lake. The sound of pounding hooves drifted toward them. He narrowed his eyes, trying to see through the tendrils of grey hovering over the water. The horses were coming around the lake, riding straight toward them.

The thundering in his heart rose to a roar, and blood pounded in his ear. He tightened his grip on his spear. His hand was sweaty and shaking. So there was to be a battle with the Eirdkilrs after all.

"I wonder who that is," said the man beside him.

Duvain frowned. There was no fear in the man's voice, only curiosity. He glanced at the men crowded at the east gate beside him. Private Kipper, one of the men who had come to the Deadheads with Captain Lingram, stood alert but not in a fighting stance. His shield rested on the ground, and his sword remained sheathed.

Duvain's eyes darted back to the horses. They'd come closer, though the mist and distance turned them into little more than blurred forms.

The horses! He cursed himself for a fool. All the tales of the Eirdkilrs told that the massive barbarians didn't ride horses. Their size made it nearly impossible for them to ride—no horse could carry Endyn or anyone nearly that large—and horses wouldn't survive in the Frozen Wastes. They had shaggy-haired, horned wild oxen that hauled their supplies, but they marched and fought on foot.

So who could the riders be?

The tightness in Duvain's gut slowly relaxed, and his tension turned to curiosity as well. He watched, transfixed, as the figures drew closer.

He got a better look at them as their horses labored up the incline toward the gate. Four men rode in a protective circle around a fifth figure. The four wore mottled brown robes, fur cloaks, and leather armor, but bore no insignia or mark of rank. Mercenaries, perhaps, or a nobleman's private guards.

The fifth man wore a cloak of costlier furs—Duvain had no idea what animals had died for that garment, but it *looked* expensive—and he rode a destrier instead of the coursers ridden by the others. The sword hanging at his hip had a gilded hilt, the sort fancied by wealthy noblemen in Einan. The scabbard showed signs of wear, and mud spattered his fancy boots, but he somehow managed to look haughty even when covered in road dust. *Definitely* a nobleman.

Captain Lingram appeared on the rampart beside him. His face tensed as he studied the approaching riders. "Open the gate," he commanded in a tight voice.

The gate swung open just as the five riders reached it. They reined in just inside, and the well-dressed rider glanced around. "Who is in command?"

"I am," Captain Lingram said, his words flat, hard.

Surprise broke through the exhaustion on the man's face. A moment later, his expression contorted, changing from fatigue and relief to a sneering snarl. "Lingram." His voice had a whiny, nasal quality, matched by the petulant look on his narrow, angular face. He would have been handsome had it not been for the large ears protruding from the mess of brown hair flopping around his face. His blue eyes were ice cold as they regarded the captain.

"Lord Virinus." Captain Lingram gave a stiff bow. "I trust the Duke's mission went well?"

A sneer twisted Lord Virinus' face. "The details of my mission are highly sensitive. What you already know is all you *need* to know."

"Of course, my lord." The captain's jaw worked. He turned to regard the men beside the gate, and his eyes rested on Duvain. "Soldier, will you escort Lord Virinus to the house prepared for him?"

69

Duvain tried not to register his surprise. "Aye, Captain!" He saluted.

Captain Lingram turned back to the nobleman. "The Fehlans have graciously made space for you in the main longhouse."

"The main longhouse?" Disdain marred Lord Virinus' face. "They expect me to room in the same place where they house their livestock and crops for the winter?"

The captain's face grew hard. "It is a rare honor for—"

"*Honor?*" The nobleman shook his head. "Call it what you will, but I will not. I expect lodgings that offer the privacy I am due as a lord of Icespire and Duke Dyrund's personal aide."

Captain Lingram, clearly struggling to control himself, nodded. "Of course, my lord." He turned to Duvain. "Soldier, Lord Virinus will be billeting in the hut where your squad is, and you will take the space in the main longhouse."

Duvain wanted to protest—Endyn would *hate* being in such a public place, where people stared at him even more than they already did—but knew better. "Yes, Captain!" With a salute, he raced toward his hut.

He banged the door open, earning a shout from Rold and a growl from Awr. Their fury only increased as he told them the reason for interrupting their rest.

"Lord Virinus?" Awr bolted upright at the nobleman's name. "Did you say *Lord Virinus?*"

Duvain nodded. "He's demanding the privacy—"

"Bloody cake-eating bastard!" Awr's sword slid from its sheath, and he stalked toward the door clad in just his boots and undertunic.

"Awr!" Rold snapped. He threw himself between his fellow corporal and the door. "Don't do anything stupid."

70

Awr glared at Rold. The fury burning in his eyes would have melted all the ice in the Frozen Sea. He was shorter but broader in the shoulder. "Move," he growled.

Rold shook his head. "Not a damned chance. We both know what'll happen if I do."

"And you think he deserves any less?" Awr demanded. "After what he did, he'd be lucky to get off with just my sword buried in his gut."

"You'd be throwing your life away," Rold insisted.

"Like you care," Awr sneered.

"Not even a little," Rold replied, "but you're one of the few men who pass for a true soldier in this place. You think I want to put my life in the hands of men like *this one*"—he jerked a thumb at Endyn, who was watching the whole thing from his bedroll—"so close to the front lines?"

Awr tightened his grip on his blade. "If you know what's good for you, Rold, you'll get the bloody hell out of my way."

Rold's eyes flicked to Awr's sword, then back to the corporal. "No."

"Keeper damn you, Rold, I'll—"

"Corporal!" Captain Lingram's voice echoed in the tiny hut.

Awr snapped to attention, his spine stiff. "Captain, sir." He saluted.

Captain Lingram strode closer, and Rold moved aside. "Do we have a problem, Corporal?"

Awr's jaw worked. "Captain…" he started.

"Corporal, let me make one thing abundantly clear." Steel echoed in the captain's voice—his tone brooked no dissent. "Our *true* orders are to protect Lord Virinus as he returns from a classified mission with Duke Dyrund. He has with him something that will prove critical in our efforts against the Eirdkilrs. Which means it's in our best interest to keep him from harm for as long as he remains under our charge." He lowered his

71

voice to a menacing growl. "Despite any personal feelings on the matter. Is that understood?"

Awr's silence dragged on for heart-pounding seconds before he replied. "Aye, Captain." Vitriol tinged his words; he could have poisoned an entire platoon with the acid in his tone.

"Good." Captain Lingram stepped back. "Now, as Duvain here said, this building will be turned over to Lord Virinus, and you will be billeted in the main longhouse."

Endyn stiffened, his expression tightening.

"Get your gear and clear out at once. You have two hours to settle in, then Sergeant Brash will be running you through drills." Captain Lingram's gaze fixed on Awr. "I trust this will be the *last* time I hear anything on this particular subject?"

Awr answered through clenched teeth. "Aye, Captain."

"Good. Then you have your orders." With a nod to Corporal Rold, he strode from the tent.

Like a good soldier, Awr went about stuffing his gear into his pack. Rold, Owen, and Weasel gave him a wide berth, but they all watched him from the corners of their eyes. The grizzled corporal kept up a steady stream of curses under his breath. "Useless as a soup sandwich" and "cake-eating ponce" counted among the kindest of words he had for Lord Virinus.

When Awr slung his pack over his shoulder, Rold hurried to do the same, and motioned for Owen to follow. Clearly they meant to keep Awr from doing anything stupid.

When the others had gone, Duvain turned to Weasel. "What was that all about?"

"Remember how I said he pissed in the wrong man's boots?" Weasel asked.

Duvain nodded.

"They were Lord Virinus' boots."

Duvain's eyes widened.

Weasel frowned. "I couldn't figure it before, but it's startin' to make sense, us comin' here. There ain't no reason this little village should matter to anyone. And it don't. We're only here to guard the toff because he's afraid of a few savages. His father's got enough clout to get a whole platoon to do his biddin'." A wry grin twisted his lips. "Not *too* much clout, though. Not enough to make Commander Galerius consider it worth sparing Ninth Company's best, even on Duke Dyrund's orders. Bloody bootless fop!" Shaking his head, he shouldered his ruck and strode from the hut.

Duvain looked over at Endyn. "How is it?" His brother moved without wincing, but Duvain knew the salve would only alleviate the discomfort for a short time.

Endyn shrugged.

Duvain drew in a breath. "Don't let it get that bad again, you hear me?"

Endyn grimaced and nodded.

"Let's go." Together, they exited the hut, their packs and bedrolls slung over their shoulders. Lord Virinus stood outside, his arms folded across his chest. Beneath his costly fur cloak, he wore dull brown clothing that still managed to look more stylish than practical. Duvain stifled a snigger as he pictured the nobleman marching in his high-heeled riding boots.

Three of his guards had dismounted and stood in a defensive position around him. Their clothes showed no trace of finery, but were the simple, utilitarian robes of fighting men. Their leather armor had been as well-maintained as the Legionnaires' mail shirts and breastplates, but they bore the marks of use. They moved with the self-confident poise of career warriors—very much at odds with the nobleman's assumed hauteur.

Lord Virinus tapped his toes. "What's the delay, Captain? After a long night of riding, I expect a bit more professionalism and alacrity than this."

Captain Lingram's expression tightened. "You may enter, my lord."

"Not much to look at," Lord Virinus muttered as he strode toward the hut. After a cursory examination, he shook his head. "Abysmal, but what choice do we have?"

He turned to one of the two guards. "Bring her."

Saluting, the guard turned back to the horses. The fourth guard had remained in his saddle. At Lord Virinus' command, he removed his heavy fur cloak. Duvain's eyes widened. A young girl sat in the saddle behind the man. Thick bands of cloth bound her to the man's back. Her long tresses were the pale yellow only seen among the Fehlan, and despite her tender age—not yet a young woman—her features were as strong and pronounced as any in Saerheim.

Duvain's mind raced. What was Lord Virinus doing with a Fehlan girl? A captive? Someone he'd found on his travels? A slave? No, that couldn't be. Slavery had been outlawed by Prince Toran of Icespire decades before. So what, then? And why was she bound to the man's saddle?

His last question was answered when the mounted man removed the straps and the girl sagged into the arms of the waiting guards. Her eyelids flickered open, but her gaze was glassy, unfocused. Sweat trickled down her face and stained her thin garments. Fever tinged her cheeks bright red, and she mumbled incoherently. She made no protest as one of the guards gathered her into his arms and carried her into the hut.

A sick Fehlan girl? Duvain's imagination ran wild. Already, the few Legionnaires within eyeshot had turned to each other, no doubt speculating about her identity.

With a scowl for Captain Lingram and the Legionnaires, Lord Virinus turned, stalked inside the hut, and slammed the door behind him.

Chapter Six

Growing up, Duvain had believed the spinsters of Northfield to be the worst gossips in Einan. With far too much time on their hands, the biddies had concocted all manner of spurious rumors: the widower blacksmith was having an affair with a visiting nobleman's wife, the mayor had a predilection for enjoying the company of his horse a bit too much, and the tanner's youngest daughter practiced witchcraft—the only explanation for the odd pox scars on her face. Even the local Beggar Priest failed to escape their notice; according to their wagging tongues, he spent donated coin on ale at the Northfield Inn rather than on caring for the poor. No tale was too small to be inflamed out of proportion, twisted, or dissected.

Those women had nothing on Legionnaires.

In the two days since Lord Virinus' arrival, every rumor had been discussed and discarded a dozen times over. Of particular interest was the girl he'd brought. Her Fehlan features left no doubt of her parentage. But if not his daughter, who *was* she? More than a few Legionnaires whispered that the nobleman's taste in women ran far too young for the people of Icespire, but the savages had no such restrictions on age. Some even wondered if she was his slave, his mistress, or a barbarian witch disguised as an innocent child.

His presence and the secrecy of his mission also received its share of argument. Many called him a spy who had penetrated deep behind enemy lines, while others insisted he was on a scouting trip studying the

Eirdkilrs' positions. His four protectors—definitely mercenaries or private guards, given their unkempt appearance and non-standard issue clothing and weapons—gave no answer to the multitude of questions. In fact, they tended to avoid most of the off-duty Legionnaires. When not standing watch before Lord Virinus' commandeered home, they spent their time amongst themselves, talking in low voices. Duvain had caught a few words of Fehlan when they spoke.

His lessons with Awr had proceeded slowly. He could exchange a few greetings in Fehlan, but little more. However, as long as he kept the liquor flowing, the grizzled corporal kept teaching him. He'd picked up a few more words while off duty in the longhouse. Elder Asmund had given Squad Three a corner of the longhouse with a bit of privacy—for which Endyn was grateful—but the constant movement of villagers in and out of the structure gave him a chance to hear them speak. Always in hushed tones, though, with wary, even suspicious glances at them.

Every member of Squad Three had pressed Awr for details on Captain Lingram's history with Lord Virinus, but he refused to expound. When questioned about Lord Virinus' mystery guest, Awr had simply said the girl was important—important enough to delay the nobleman's travels as she convalesced. Whether he knew more or remained as in the dark as they, he didn't let on.

That proved the only sliver of excitement or intrigue in what had become very long, very boring days. Sergeant Brash began their days with a thorough examination of their quarters, followed by a detailed inspection of their armor and weapons. Failure to meet his exacting standards resulted in either an additional turn at watch or an extra-brutal training session.

Before morning chow—decent food, thanks to the villagers providing meat, vegetables, and grains from their meager stores— Corporal Awr pushed them through a ruck march. They trooped around the village in full armor, packs loaded on their backs. When Awr was in a truly foul mood—a lot more common since Lord Virinus' arrival—he'd take them a full three leagues through dense forest, thick brush, and muddy trails. By end of the first day, Duvain had come to dread the end of their march. Awr vented his frustration by setting them running up the steep hill beyond the east gate. On the last run, Duvain would have fainted if not for Rold's hand on his back, pushing him onward. Endyn didn't fare much better. His brother fatigued quickly, and Squads Two and Three had done hundreds of push-ups—in full armor and their packs—Awr's sadistic way of encouraging Endyn to recover from his exhaustion faster.

Meal times gave them a few minutes to recover before the endless base duties: fortifying the palisade ramparts, digging ditches and latrines, cleaning their cramped quarters, and providing muscle power for whatever tasks the villagers needed to prepare Saerheim for the coming winter.

Then came the drills. Oh, so many drills! Formation practice bled into quick-time marches, rapid redirectioning, and recovery from a collapsed shield wall. Awr and Rold usually spent their last hour of training hammering tactics into their heads, then finished with extra weapons practice. On the bad days, they'd spend another hour marching at top speed. Stragglers would be left in the dense forests to find their own way back to the village.

Thankfully, the quality of the evening meal had improved over the dinners served back at Icespire. The villagers grew their own herbs and spices, and one of the mess officers even spoke enough of the Fehlan tongue to learn a few Saerheim tricks for turning dried meat, stale bread, and withered root vegetables into surprisingly edible meals.

If they were lucky, they had an hour or two of personal time—usually spent polishing, sharpening, and mending their gear. Awr lost himself in the bottom of a wineskin or mug of ale whenever possible. Weasel, Owen, and Rold diced and gambled. Endyn joined in whenever they allowed him, but retreated when they stared as if he'd infect them with his dragonskin. Duvain had tried in vain to explain that the condition wasn't contagious. They'd simply given *him* the cold shoulder as well.

The rest of the Deadheads were friendly enough. They invited him and Endyn to gamble, drink, and swap stories with them, though they still shot odd glances at Endyn. The fact that he'd survived a woodcutter viper's bite made him phenomenon enough, but Duvain suspected Weasel or Rold had talked about Endyn's condition.

Every man in Ninth Company stood one of the three eight-hour watch shifts. Most of the Legionnaires in the other four squads hated night shift, but Duvain preferred it. The chill cooled Endyn's skin, preventing the dragonskin from growing worse. Though the armor still rubbed the skin raw, at least he didn't have to worry about sweating. However, some nights grew terribly cold, exacerbating the pain of the dragonskin.

Tonight, Squad Three had evening watch, which ended at midnight. Duvain, on patrol of the south wall with Endyn, caught a glimpse of Captain Lingram sitting in the main square. The captain was talking with Elder Asmund and sharing a cup of *drikke*—a potent brew made of fermented malt, hops, yeast, juniper boughs, and sugar. The captain appeared relaxed, at ease with Elder Asmund, speaking in Fehlan. Duvain only caught occasional snatches of their conversation but understood none of it.

Duvain wasn't the only one watching the captain. Lord Virinus stood at the door of his hut, his gaze fixed on the two men lounging in the main square. Even from this distance, Duvain caught the unmistakable venom in his expression. Duvain had noticed that Lord Virinus' eyes followed the captain's movements. Just as Awr's glare tracked the nobleman.

"What do you think," Weasel was asking as Duvain and Endyn reached the brazier at the northeast corner of the wall. "After nearly a week sittin' around holdin' our pricks and doin' piss-all, I find myself wondering what's so important we got dragged all the way out here. Not that I mind a lot of doin' nothin', but I'd rather be doin' it back in camp, or behind the walls of Dagger Garrison."

Owen said nothing. He sat on the wooden rampart, reclined against the wall, a faraway look in his eyes as he stared at the fire. His fingers toyed with a silver sword pendant hanging from a leather thong about his neck.

Weasel scowled. "Hey, taintwad!" He snapped his fingers in front of Owen's eyes.

Owen jerked upright. "What?"

Weasel shook his head. "Snap out of it before Sarge thinks you're nappin' on watch."

"I wasn't sleeping," Owen said in a heavy voice.

Weasel rolled his eyes. "Lemme guess, thinkin' about your *girl* again?"

Owen nodded.

"She give you that?" Weasel asked, indicating the pendant with his chin.

Owen glanced down and nodded. "Her father taught her to pray to the Swordsman."

"God of heroes." Weasel snorted.

"God of war, too." Owen's brow furrowed. "Said it would keep me safe."

Weasel rolled his eyes. "Yes, a piece of bleedin' metal is going to keep the barbarians' swords from guttin' you."

Owen's face hardened. "At least I *have* someone to pray to, someone to respect. No doubt you're too good for the gods."

Weasel shook his head. "Not at all. I just never had much use for heroism. Now, the Watcher in the Dark, god of the night, patron of thieves, that's a god worth talkin' to."

"Patron of thieves?" Duvain's eyebrows rose. "I thought the Watcher was the god of justice."

Weasel shrugged. "To some people he is. I prefer him as the face of vengeance. More poetic, that way." He fixed Duvain with a hard look. "Don't tell me you buy into all that rubbish about the Swordsman, too? Endyn?"

Endyn shook his head and produced a small crown-shaped pendant made of iron. Duvain had one to match; they'd been the last gift from their mother, who had instilled in them a reverence for the Master, god of virtue and nobility. Though she'd been as lowborn as anyone in

79

the little village of Northfield, she'd had an inner dignity that would have belonged in any court on Einan.

"Mock all you want," Owen said, "but I'll keep it if it means a better chance of getting home to her safe."

"How long has it been?" Weasel asked, his tone surprisingly free of mockery.

Owen sighed. "Two years, eight months, and two days." His brow furrowed. "I'm starting to forget what she looks like."

"Might be for the best," Weasel said. "You know how these things go. Woman promises a man she'll wait. Man goes off to war, comes home a hero and finds woman in bed with his neighbor. And his neighbor's brother."

Duvain raised an eyebrow at the oddly specific detail.

Weasel threw up his hands. "I'm just sayin', you may want to think about findin' yourself a new dame once you get home. You'll have enough Icespire coin in your pocket to get any girl."

Owen shook his head. "I don't want any girl. I want Issala."

"Name like that, she's definitely imaginary." A vulpine grin spread Weasel's rat face. "Or a horse-faced nag."

Owen scowled. "She was the prettiest girl in the Merchant's Quarter. All the other men were after her, but she picked me. Her father, though…"

"Didn't want her marryin' a penniless git like you, eh?" Weasel nodded. "Oldest tale in the book."

"Not at all," Owen said. "Her father didn't care that I didn't have money. But he said he could never let his daughter marry a man who hadn't served his city with pride. He was a Legionnaire himself. Fought at Garrow's Canyon. With our captain, actually."

"Wait, you said you're from Praamis?" Weasel asked, and Owen nodded. "And your girl's pa was one of the only *four* men to walk away from Garrow's Canyon?"

Again, Owen nodded.

"Keeper's icy teats!" Weasel whistled. "You're dreamin' about the daughter of Tiaban Bloodfist, a bona fide war hero? I underestimated you, I did."

Owen gave him a sad smile. "Can't marry her as long as I'm on this side of the Frozen Sea. I still have two of my four years left to serve."

"Damn!" Weasel shook his head. "That's a long time to wait."

Owen nodded. "It is, but she's worth it."

"If her old man's the Bloodfist, you're damn right she is." Weasel settled back into a comfortable position. "You'd never pay for a drink again, marryin' into a military legacy like that."

"Scouts returning!" Rold called from his perch atop the ramparts. "Squad Three, get that gate open."

Owen, Weasel, Duvain, and Endyn rushed to the eastern gate. With effort, they lifted the heavy locking bar and swung one massive gate open. The two scouts trotted through with a nod of thanks, but didn't stop until they reached Captain Lingram.

"I wonder what news they're bringing," Duvain pondered aloud.

Weasel snorted. "Like as not, a whole fat lot of nothin'. We're way behind the front, with an entire army between us and the bastard savages. The worst thing we've got to worry about is the whorefrost." He grinned. "Too bloody cold, and if you fall asleep in her arms, there's a good chance you'll end up dead."

Owen shook his head. "Not that you'd know. There isn't a whore in the Beggar's Quarter that would come within a league of that diseased lump of flesh you call a prick."

Weasel grinned. "Tarts ain't my type, Owen. Ask anyone."

Owen rolled his eyes. "You sleep with *one* general's wife, and you suddenly think you're the Mistress' gift to women."

Both Duvain's and Endyn's eyebrows shot up, which only made Weasel's grin broaden.

"It's how he got his name," Owen said with a disdainful shake of his head. "In all the battles he's fought, he's somehow managed not to get dead. Slippery as a weasel, and about as trustworthy, too. He'll shag any woman within thirty paces—and that's using the term 'woman' generously."

"Your mother didn't seem to mind it," Weasel retorted.

The insult rolled off Owen without effect. "Look, I get you're nervous," he told Duvain. "Even this far from enemy territory, it's normal for a tenderfoot to get a bit antsy. That's why we're on watch, and that's why the scouts go out. The Legion's trained to prepare for anything. But even Captain Lingram will tell you there's not much out here that can kill you besides bears and snakes."

"That, and our bloody Lord Virinus." Weasel's face creased into a scowl. "I'll be keepin' out of his way, thank you very much."

Duvain nodded and leaned against the wall, listening to the sound of Weasel and Owen's conversation. They were right. He was worrying for nothing. He chalked it up to the nervousness of inexperience. But after long minutes of trying to relax, he couldn't.

He got to his feet with a groan. "If it's all the same to you, I'll do another round of the walls. Just to be sure."

Weasel gave him a dismissive wave. "Suit yourself! If it gets you to shut up and stop worryin', do what you have to."

Duvain climbed onto the palisade ramparts and strode along its length. His eyes searched the shadows of the forest for any signs of life. He occasionally thought he spotted movement, but it always proved to be the leaves and branches blown in the chill evening wind. Tension knotted his shoulders. Yet no matter how hard he stared, the nagging doubts in his mind proved unfounded.

There was nothing to fear out there.

Endyn winced as he set down his breastplate and reached for his helmet. He'd made a right turn when Sergeant Brash shouted to wheel left, and had earned a shield rim in the ribs for his effort. The sergeant's reprimand had been quiet but effective. Endyn hadn't made a mistake the rest of the practice.

Duvain tried not to think about his own failures. He'd started to get the hang of marching in the shield wall and moving in time with the shouted orders, but he still had a long way to go before he'd feel ready for battle. The disdain in Rold's eyes cemented that belief.

Weasel looked up from where he sat, working on his own gear. A sly grin twisted his face. "You may be rubbish in the shield wall, big man, but, by the Keeper, you polish your helmet with the best of them!"

Endyn stared down at his helm, then back up at Weasel. A moment later, understanding dawned, and his face turned a dark scarlet.

Weasel snickered, and Rold and Owen added their chuckles. Endyn ducked his head and focused on his task, but the harder he worked, the more Weasel laughed. Face aflame, he set aside the helmet and reached for his boot.

He dropped the boot and leapt to his feet with an uncharacteristic cry, eyes wide. Duvain's pulse spiked in alarm. Were they under attack? A moment later, his worry faded as a hideous creature crawled from Endyn's boot. Long, segmented, with scores of tiny legs and vicious pincers, the critter's bite could cause swelling, fever, chills, weakness, and, in some cases, even proved fatal.

Weasel's mirth turned to full-bellied guffaws. Endyn's eyes darted between the centipede and the small Legionnaire, his face darkening. Seeing Endyn's expression, Weasel darted from the longhouse and out into the main square, laughter echoing in his wake. With a scowl and shake of his head, Rold set aside his armor and stalked out of the longhouse.

Endyn's fists clenched and relaxed, and he sucked in great angry breaths through his nostrils. Duvain hadn't seen his brother this furious since the time Mal the miller's son had blackened his eye. In his rage, Endyn had nearly snapped the older boy's spine. His brother had been fourteen at the time—now, at his full size and strength, he'd crush Weasel's head in his huge hands without breaking a sweat.

Owen spoke first. "Easy, big guy." He looked up from his polishing, a little smile on his face. "Pranks like this don't deserve a beating—they deserve a bit of *payback*."

Endyn's brows knit. "What?" he rumbled. "What do you mean?"

Owen set aside his breastplate and reached for his mail shirt. "Weasel's earned a thrashing, but that'll just get you in trouble. Brawling's forbidden in the Legion, especially when it comes to someone of your size pounding on a needle-prick like Weasel. But nowhere in the regulations is it forbidden from getting a bit of justice in your own way. As long as it's not flashy and doesn't keep Weasel from standing shift or drilling, you can get creative."

Endyn's expression grew pensive, and he returned to his seat to resume his care of his equipment. Duvain caught his brother's eye and raised an eyebrow. Endyn gave a little smile. Clearly, vengeance against Weasel *would* come—they just needed to figure out how.

The sound of a clearing throat drew his attention upward. A white-haired woman stood at the boundary of the space they'd marked for the Legion, just within the curtain of hanging furs that offered a modicum of privacy.

Duvain had seen her before. She had to be at least in her eighth decade, her back slightly stooped, yet she moved with speed and grace that belied her. Her hands were always moving, her eyes darting around. He didn't need to speak the Fehlan tongue to recognize the tone of command in her voice.

She rattled off a string of words in her language. Duvain searched for Awr, but the grizzled corporal had gone in search of drink rather than care for his gear. Only Owen and Endyn remained beside him.

He fumbled for the few words he'd learned. He stammered out what he hoped was a greeting in Fehlan—either that, or he'd just bid her farewell.

The old woman rolled her eyes, and the acid in her voice made her opinion on his grasp of the Fehlan tongue plain. She said something in her sharp, curt tone.

Duvain didn't understand a single word. He shook his head. "I'm sorry, I—"

She thrust something at him: a wooden bowl, containing a thick green paste that reeked of herbs, spices, and something earthy. His brow furrowed. What did she want him to do with it?

She thrust a gnarled finger at the bowl, then at Endyn.

"For him?" Duvain indicated Endyn.

The woman nodded. She patted her chest and pointed at the paste once more.

Duvain's eyes widened. Endyn had tried to hide his dragonskin from the villagers, but the wide-open longhouse offered little privacy. More than a few of the people of Saerheim, including Elder Asmund, had caught glimpses of the thick grey scales. Yet the Fehlans' reaction lacked the disgust of the Legionnaires. They saw him as an oddity—he was far taller than any Princelander, taller even than the Eirdkilrs, and had the strange incrustation covering his body—but not something to be shunned. No more so than the rest of the men who had invaded their village.

Duvain mimed applying the cream to his chest. The woman nodded and thrust the bowl at him again.

He took it and bowed. "Thank you."

The woman gave him a smile, revealing three white teeth among a sea of pink gums. With a final string of Fehlan words Duvain didn't understand, she disappeared into the shadows of the longhouse.

A small shadow remained in her wake: a boy, no older than four or five, peeked from behind a hanging fur, his grey eyes wide in curiosity.

85

Duvain smiled and waved. The boy squeaked and fled after the retreating matriarch.

Chuckling, Duvain turned to Endyn. "Hey, look at this." He held out the bowl. "They made it for you."

Endyn sniffed at the bowl and recoiled with disgust.

"Not to eat, idiot!" Duvain rolled his eyes. He motioned to Endyn's chest. "For the dragonskin."

Endyn's eyebrows shot up. "Are you sure?" he rumbled. "Is it safe?"

Duvain studied the paste. The potent mixture of herbs and spices made his eyes water, but he had no idea what it contained. After a moment of hesitation, he shrugged. "I don't know. But if they were trying to poison us, I doubt they'd start with the two lowest-ranking Deadheads."

Endyn's expression remained dubious.

"Your call, Brother, but maybe it can help?" Duvain met his brother's gaze. Endyn had been forcing a brave face, but Duvain knew the truth: the dragonskin was worsening. The patches of scaled skin grew thicker every day, and the Sanctuary healers' ointment hadn't prevented the painful cracks and inflammation.

With a sigh, Endyn nodded. "Do it."

Owen looked up as Endyn struggled with his shirt. His face turned a shade of pale, but he offered, "Here, let me help."

Endyn's face darkened, but he made no protest as Owen helped him tug the tunic over his head.

Duvain scooped up a small amount of the paste. "Tell me if this stuff hurts." He applied a thin layer to a small section of Endyn's back where the cracked skin was red and inflamed. The smell of infection had grown stronger.

"How's that?" Owen asked, genuine concern in his eyes.

86

Endyn hissed. "Burns a little." After a moment, however, the tension in his face dissipated. "Huh. Better."

Duvain stared down at the paste with interest. He sniffed it again. He'd *have* to ask the old woman for the recipe.

As he covered Endyn's back with the stuff, he noticed a burning sensation in his hands. The sting grew more painful with every passing minute. By the time he'd finished, his hands were red and felt hot and sensitive to the touch.

He'd experienced that sensation once before: he'd made the foolish mistake of rubbing his eyes after eating the spicy red peppers his mother grew in her herb garden. Something in those peppers burned not only the tongue, but the skin as well. The more sensitive the skin, the stronger the burn.

He glanced down at his hands, at Endyn's boot, and back up at his brother. A slow smile spread his face. "I think I've just found out how we get back at Weasel."

Endyn's rumbling chuckle brought a lightness to Duvain's chest. It felt good to see his brother smile after so much pain.

Chapter Seven

"Keeper take it, Weasel!" Rold snarled. "If you need to relieve yourself, just drop your britches and get on with it."

"I-I'm fine, Corporal." Sweat trickled down Weasel's forehead. He'd shifted back and forth for the last fifteen minutes, his face growing redder by the second. "Really."

Duvain did his best not to look at Weasel. If he did, he knew he'd burst out laughing.

"If you were fine, you nob-gobbling buffoon, you wouldn't be hopping around like a one-legged nitwit at an ass-kicking party." Rold's face went hard. "Is there something you'd like to explain to me, soldier?"

"No, Corporal." Weasel shook his head, but his face had taken on a desperate expression. After another long minute of wiggling, he'd had enough. "Keeper's twisted gobnards, it burns!" With this, he ripped off his breeches and underwear and, tackle flapping in the wind, raced toward a nearby longhouse. He thrust his hands into one of the barrels set to collect rainwater falling off the eaves and splashed water frantically over his crotch.

Endyn's snort turned into a rumbling chuckle. Duvain elbowed him, but struggled to discipline his own expression. Rold shot the pair of them a suspicious glance. "You two know what's going on?"

"No, Corporal!" Duvain said. "Might be those diseases are finally getting the best of him."

Corporal Rold's brow furrowed. "Or someone put something in Weasel's underwear."

"Might be that, too, sir." Duvain plastered his most innocent expression. "Can't truly say for certain."

After a moment, the severity on Rold's face gave way to a smile. "Fair enough, meat."

"You bastards!" Weasel shouted. Judging by the water splashed over his boots and the sodden ground beneath him, he'd emptied nearly a quarter of the enormous barrel. "I know it was one of you tossers. When I find out who did it—"

He swallowed his words as Captain Lingram emerged from the longhouse where he'd been billeted. With a look of pure horror, face going pale as a corpse, Weasel raced out of the captain's eyesight, toward the back entrance to their longhouse. Duvain had never seen anyone run so fast.

Deep in conversation with one of the two scouts, Captain Lingram either didn't notice Weasel or pretended not to. After a brief exchange, the scout saluted and strode toward his horse. Captain Lingram watched the man ride out of the gate, then turned toward their guard post.

"Squad Three, it seems Sergeant Brash has taken pity on you and given you the morning watch."

Corporal Rold saluted. "Aye, Captain. Either that, or the pricks of Squad Five pissed him off worse than we did."

"As you say." He lifted his eyes to Endyn. "How fares your health, soldier?"

Endyn, surprised by the captain's interest, managed to rumble out, "F-Fine, sir."

"Good," Captain Lingram said, but without really listening. His brow had a deep line down the middle. He seemed distracted, out of sorts. He usually paid attention to everything around him, yet now his eyes never focused on anything.

"Is everything well, Captain?" Duvain asked.

"What's that?" Captain Lingram looked up, and the light returned to his eyes. "Oh, yes, of course." He nodded.

The captain's distraction worried Duvain. Something had to be seriously wrong to make Captain Lingram look worried. But he didn't know the captain well enough to persist.

Without another word to them, the captain strode away.

"It's bad." Awr's rasping voice sounded quietly from behind them. "I don't know what's got under his skin, but he only gets like that when the sky's about to break open and piss acid."

"But what could it be?" Rold demanded. "You heard the last scouting report, just like I did. Not even a hint of any Eirdkilrs in Deid lands. Until we receive word from Commander Galerius, we continue on as commanded."

"Might be that's it," Awr said. "Galerius is competent enough, but the Eirdkilrs are smart. Captain may know something we—"

"You Keeper-damned useless heathen witch!" A high-pitched shout cut off Awr's words. "You're trying to *poison* her!"

All eyes darted toward the small hut, and to the elegantly-clad figure stomping out the front door. Lord Virinus held the old woman by the arm, dragging her along behind him. She looked like a cornered wildcat, protesting and spitting what could only be Fehlan curses. With a vicious snarl, the nobleman shoved the old woman. She stumbled but caught herself nimbly and unleashed a fresh torrent of angry words on him.

Lord Virinus waved a slim finger in her face. "I bring her to you to *heal* her, and all you've done is make things worse with your ridiculous potions and poultices and witchcraft."

The old woman—the village healer, Duvain had learned—was uncowed by Lord Virinus' rage. Though she barely reached his chest, she had no problem squaring off with him, meeting his anger with an acerbic stream of Fehlan that needed no translation.

"My lord!" A breathless Captain Lingram raced toward them. "My lord, what is the matter?"

Lord Virinus rounded on the captain, his tone apoplectic. "This savage is killing my guest. She—"

"Lord Virinus." Captain Lingram cut off the nobleman with a voice hard as iron. "While I can appreciate your concerns, remember where we are."

"Wading in the mud and filth of barbarians and ignorants!" Lord Virinus' voice rose to a shout.

"We are in *their* home," Captain Lingram said, "where they have done nothing but welcome us and provide us the best they can."

"The *best?*" The nobleman's voice turned shrill. "I haven't had a proper meal in the last week, and I sleep on a mat of reeds rather than a real bed. Under any other circumstances, this would be an insult!"

"But we aren't under other circumstances." The captain spoke in a cold, calm voice. "We have each been given a command by our superiors, and we are to make the best of the situation. Which I took to mean accepting the hospitality of our allies and *not* insulting their revered elders."

"It's no insult if it is the truth!" Lord Virinus shouted. "After all this time, the girl has shown no sign of recovering. That…that *crone* has spent every day applying one foul brew or poultice after another, to no effect. If anything, the girl is getting worse. The way things are going, she'll wind up dead long before Duke Dyrund's rider reaches us!"

For the first time, it seemed he noticed the crowd of Legionnaires that had gathered—soldiers loved anything that distracted them from the drudgery of their mundane rituals. "And do your men have nothing better to do than stand around lolly-gagging?"

Captain Lingram turned and nodded to the assorted Legionnaires. "Back to work, or back to your tasks, men. This doesn't concern you." He turned back to Lord Virinus. "I'd be happy to listen to your concerns, my lord, but perhaps somewhere more private?" He gestured toward the small, muddy track that ran between Lord Virinus' hut and the northern longhouse.

With a snort, the nobleman stomped off. Captain Lingram followed, his expression as tight as his stiff shoulders.

Owen and Endyn returned their attention to their post at the northwest corner of the wall, but Weasel turned to Duvain. "Seems like a good time to patrol along the north wall, doesn't it?" He winked. "Never know what sort of enemies could be hidin' out there."

Duvain understood. He shot a questioning glance at Rold.

The corporal nodded. "Good thinking, Private. Keep your *eyes* open."

With a crisp salute, Weasel began to march eastward along north wall—toward to the place where Captain Lingram and Lord Virinus stood arguing.

"…must understand who she is, Captain," Lord Virinus was saying in a clipped tone. "Eirik Throrsson is more than just the leader of clan *Fjall*—he is the *only* one who might unite the rest of the clans against the Eirdkilrs. The future of the war depends on this alliance. Duke Dyrund went to great lengths to make peace with the *Fjall*. It is only by the Minstrel's mercy that I was not struck down by the same fever that claimed him, half our escort, and soon the *Hilmir's* daughter. Were that to happen, calling it a diplomatic fiasco would be the understatement of the epoch."

"I can appreciate that, my lord." Captain Lingram inclined his head. "What you and the Duke have accomplished with Throrsson is truly admirable. His wisdom will be sorely missed."

Lord Virinus' lips pressed into a thin line, and he scanned the captain's expression as if expecting an insult hidden in those words.

Captain Lingram's face could have been carved from stone. "With the Duke's passing, *you* are the Prince's envoy to the Fehlans. And we are among the *Deid*, the oldest of our Fehlan allies. Insulting one of their elders would be like slapping Prince Toran in the face."

Lord Virinus' eyes narrowed. "Nonsense!"

"If you've spent time among the Fehlans, my lord," Captain Lingram replied in a voice that made it clear he expected Lord Virinus had *not* done so, "you will know how they venerate their elders. Eira is considered one of the greatest healers not only among the people of Saerheim, but *all* of clan Deid."

Lord Virinus snorted. "Bloody Minstrel have mercy!"

Captain Lingram didn't dignify that with an answer. "Your frustrations at our guest's wellbeing are valid, but we must remember that we are in Saerheim, not Icespire."

The nobleman ground his teeth. "Very well, Captain." The words came out in an almost-sneer. "If you feel so strongly about it, *you* smooth things over with the natives." He shook a finger in the captain's face. "But mark my words, that crone isn't coming near Branda again! *No one* sees her until the Duke's rider arrives."

The captain shrugged. "I will relay your message to Elder Asmund and Eira." With a stiff nod, he turned and strode toward the main longhouse.

Duvain kept his eyes fixed straight ahead and did his best to keep his pace even. The last thing he needed was to attract the ire of Lord Virinus. He and Weasel reached the northeast corner of the wall, turned, and marched back to Corporal Rold at the northwest.

"Well?"

Weasel relayed the information they'd gleaned from the captain's conversation.

"By the Watcher," growled Rold. "Branda, the daughter of Eirik Throrsson? If the *Fjall* join the war against the Eirdkilrs—"

"Things would end a lot more quickly," Weasel finished. "But if she dies…" He drew his thumb across his throat.

"The most powerful clan leader in Fehlan history becomes our enemy." For the first time, genuine fear echoed in Rold's voice. He made the sign of the Watcher. "Keeper have mercy on us if that day ever comes."

* * *

Duvain labored under the weight of his two packs. His own armor and ruck weighed enough to slow him down, but Sergeant Brash, in a particularly foul mood, had loaded them all up with double weight. They'd barely marched five hundred paces from camp, but already fatigue threatened to drag him to the ground.

"Company, shield wall!" Sergeant Brash shouted. "Spear formation."

Squad Three weren't alone in their misery. Sergeant Brash had dragged Squads Two and Four along for good measure. Squad Five only escaped by merit of snoring the day away after a long midnight shift. Squad One had called out insults and gibes from their position on the ramparts. More than one marching Legionnaire had growled at the "lucky bastards on watch".

With the three squads, thirty-two men stood in the shield wall. Sergeant Brash barked out the orders from ahead of the line, while the sergeants of Squads Two and Four snapped and snarled at any Legionnaire too slow to respond to commands.

With an exhausted groan, Duvain hitched up the packs and struggled to take his place in line without losing his grip on his shield and spear. He shook his head as Endyn tried to help support the load. The last thing his brother needed was to piss off Sergeant Brash any more than he already had. Endyn's performance in the last few drill sessions had not improved.

The sergeant loved to push them to their limits. When on forced marches, he'd wait until they were exhausted, then order them to form a shield line and advance in tight formation. During line drills, he'd have them fast-march in every direction until their legs ached and they couldn't remember which way they were originally headed. He'd call new formations, speeds, and patterns of movement before they'd finished forming up the last one.

Duvain understood the need for such drills—after all, they needed to be prepared to face any enemy anywhere—but basic training had been nowhere near as challenging. The exertion had strengthened his muscles, but his body suffered under the strain. He was one mistake away from snapping. Or collapsing.

Endyn tripped over his own feet and stumbled forward. His hewing spear knocked off Weasel's helmet, and his massive knee struck Owen in the back.

"Keeper take it!" Weasel shouted, whirling on Endyn. "When are you goin' to learn—?"

"Easy, Weasel." Owen interposed himself, rubbing his back. "Give him a break."

Weasel's voice rose. "A break? What the bloody hell for?" He snarled up at Endyn. "There's no way you're a Deadhead. You're not even fit to be a Legionnaire."

Endyn mumbled an apology, but Weasel launched into a tirade, cussing him out for his uselessness. Sergeant Brash made no move to stop the tongue-lashing. When Weasel finally ran out of insults, all the sergeant said was, "Back in line, soldier."

Red-faced, eyes downcast, Endyn took his place beside Duvain.

"How the Keeper's name did he even get into the Legion?" Weasel muttered in a voice loud enough for Endyn to hear.

"Forward march, double time!" Sergeant Brash shouted. He'd abandoned the shield wall practice…for now. No doubt he'd spring it on them again when they least expected it.

As they marched, Duvain felt himself flagging. His shoulders ached, his lungs burned, and his head began to spin. He couldn't keep it up much longer, not with the double load.

"Embrace the suck, soldier," Rold muttered behind him. "Fight through it, or you're nothing more than an air thief and don't deserve to wear Legion colors."

The corporal's words caught Duvain by surprise. Beneath the insult, there was genuine concern for his wellbeing. Rold actually wanted him to succeed.

Gritting his teeth, he forced himself onward. One foot in front of the other, though it felt as if molten lead filled his legs. He'd get through this hell one Keeper-damned step at a time.

"Company, halt!"

At the sergeant's shout, Duvain's head snapped up. They'd come around a bend in the forest track. A short distance away, a team of draft horses struggled to pull a wagon free of the thick mud.

"Ho, Deadheads!" shouted one of the two Legion guards accompanying the wagon. "Give us a hand, won't you?"

"Got yourselves stuck again, Eltin?" Rold shouted. "That's the third time this week, way I hear it."

The Legionnaire Eltin scowled. "Just for that, I'll make sure the quartermaster gives you a tankard of piss instead of ale."

Sergeant Brash turned to them. "Company, rest!" he called.

With a groan, Duvain dropped his two packs and sagged to the ground, uncaring of the mud seeping into his breeches. He was just glad to be free of his burden.

"On your feet, meat!" Sergeant Brash shouted.

Duvain's heart sank. The sergeant stared at him, his eyes cold and hard. He marched toward Duvain and crouched beside him. "Last one to the gate, first one to the heavy lifting." He only shouted when giving orders, yet every Legionnaire feared his quiet, calm voice.

Duvain wanted to weep. He had nothing left—he doubted he could even stand, much less march over to the wagon and be of any use.

Sergeant Brash's eyes held no mercy. "On your feet." His eyes were cold, dangerous. "Now."

Duvain struggled to rise. Every muscle in his body protested. Tears of frustration and anger brimmed in his eyes. It felt as if he lifted the weight of the world on his shoulders as he fought to one knee, then…

A huge hand rested on his shoulder. Endyn shook his head. "I've got it." Dropping his pack beside Duvain, he strode toward the mired wagon.

"Get back in line, soldier." Sergeant Brash stepped in front of Endyn. "I gave your brother an order."

"Let me do it, Sergeant," Endyn rumbled. "Please."

Sergeant Brash locked eyes with the big Legionnaire. "Is that how this is, meat?" He spoke to Duvain without taking his gaze from Endyn. "Are you that weak you're willing to let your brother here carry your burden for you?"

Duvain realized Sergeant Brash spoke to him. "No, Sergeant." He staggered to his feet, but Endyn whirled—a startling movement from one so large—and shook his head. Duvain yielded to the drag of his pack and sagged again.

"Let me, Sergeant." Endyn's thick voice carried across the line of Deadheads.

"Let anyone do it, Sergeant!" Eltin called. "We're burning daylight here."

Sergeant Brash narrowed his eyes. "You sure you want to do this, meat?" His voice held a dangerous tone.

Endyn nodded. "I've got this."

"So be it." Sergeant Brash stepped aside. "You've got it. Alone."

Duvain's eyes widened. Barrels, crates, and boxes of supplies were piled high on the back of the wagon. The load required two enormous draft horses to haul it, and all their struggles had failed to drag the wagon out of the muck. "But Sergeant—"

"Sit your candy ass down, soldier!" Brash's voice was cold, hard. "You let your brother fight your battles for you, so by the Swordsman, he's going to fight it."

Endyn didn't hesitate. Squaring his shoulders, he lumbered toward the rear of the wagon and gripped the wagon's backboard in his huge hands.

"Eltin, get your boys out of there," Sergeant Brash called.

"What's that now?" Eltin said, his expression puzzled.

"Big man's going to haul the wagon out of the muck for you. Isn't that right, soldier?" The sergeant didn't need to sneer—the utter absence of expression conveyed his disdain to perfection.

Endyn nodded. "Yes, Sergeant."

Sergeant Brash took the lead reins of the draft horses and waved Eltin away. "We've got this."

Eltin exchanged glances with his fellow Legionnaire and the three teamsters riding with the wagon. They shrugged and stepped aside.

"Suit yourself," Eltin said. "Just get it done before nightfall, eh? I've got a schedule to keep."

The sergeant gave him a withering glare, and Eltin snapped his mouth shut.

"You ready, soldier?" Brash called out.

Endyn nodded.

"Push." The single word, spoken in a quiet voice, came out so cold and hard it could have been cut from the icebergs floating in the Frozen Sea.

The sergeant tugged on the lead rope, and the draft horses leaned into their traces. Endyn's face reddened with the exertion as he shoved, and a groan escaped his lips.

The wagon didn't budge.

"Again," Sergeant Brash said in the same low tone.

Teeth gritted, spine arching, Endyn pushed once more. The muscles on his forearms corded with the effort. Still, the wagon remained firmly mired. Duvain sucked in a breath as Endyn's boots slipped on the muddy ground. His rear foot flew out and he fell to one knee, gasping for breath.

"No man wins a fight alone," Sergeant Brash said. "You succeed and fail as a unit. Every man carries their weight, or we all die."

Sweat trickled down Endyn's flushed face. His eyes were closed, and he sucked in deep breaths. Yet his expression remained unyielding. Duvain had met few men who could challenge his brother's stubbornness. He simply refused to quit—he'd done so when his father worked him harder than any of the other farmhands, and he did so now. Climbing to his feet, he dug his toes into the muddy ground, filled his lungs, and threw his weight against the wagon once more.

Shaking his head, Sergeant Brash tugged on the lead reins. The horses added their weight and strength to Endyn's effort. Nothing. A low rumble echoed from Endyn's throat, growing louder and stronger until it rose to a roar.

Duvain's heart stopped. Endyn was overexerting himself. He couldn't take the strain much longer. He couldn't—

With a wet sucking sound, the wagon wheels rolled free of the mire.

"Bugger me sideways!" Weasel muttered. Rold and Owen drew in sharp breaths.

Endyn sagged to his knees, his arms and head hanging down.

Exhaustion forgotten, Duvain rushed toward his brother. Owen appeared on the other side, lending his support to the huge man.

"You idiot!" Duvain whispered in Endyn's ear. "Why'd you do that?"

Endyn looked up with a tired smile. "Mother made me promise to look out for you."

Duvain swallowed. Their mother had been the only good thing in their young lives. She'd sheltered them from their father's wrath, wiped away Endyn's tears when the boys of Northfield called him "freak" or "monster". Even now, from beyond the grave, she looked after them. He gripped his brother's shoulder and helped him lumber around the wagon.

Endyn moved slowly. The exertion had taken a toll on him. Duvain feared his brother would collapse if he let go of him—the healers of the Sanctuary had warned against such effort. His heart, as enlarged as the rest of him, couldn't bear the strain.

But Endyn didn't collapse. He stopped in front of Sergeant Brash, who remained standing at the head of the wagon, the lead rope still in his hands.

Endyn straightened to his full towering height. "Permission to return to the line, Sergeant," he said.

Sergeant Brash nodded.

With a salute, Endyn, Duvain, and Owen marched toward the column of Legionnaires and took their place in the marching line. With effort, he shouldered his pack. Though his shoulders drooped, he held his head high.

After a moment, Sergeant Brash returned to the head of the column. "Enough for one day," he said quietly. "Back to camp."

Without a word, the column of Legionnaires made an about-face and began the short march back to the village.

Duvain spoke in a voice pitched for Weasel's ears. "Still wondering why he made it into the Legion, Weasel?"

For once, the little man had no reply.

* * *

"Aren't you goin' to share any of that?" Weasel asked.

Awr ignored him and continued emptying the wineskin. He'd bartered for it—well, *Duvain* had worked for it—with the quartermaster, and he seemed disinclined to spare even a drop.

"Come on, Awr," Weasel whined. "All we've got is this rancid goat's milk." He shook his cup, sloshing the pale white liquid.

"Not rancid," Owen said, rolling his eyes. "Fermented."

Duvain took a sip from his cup. The pungent *ayrag*, made from fermented goat or cow's milk, left a taste of almonds on his tongue. He vastly preferred it to the ale back at Icespire, but it couldn't hold a candle to a Nyslian vintage or a good Voramian Snowblossom wine.

Endyn sat in silence a short distance from the group. He had emptied his tankard long ago, and was lost in thought, his eyes fixed on the ground.

"He's a bit of an odd one, ain't he?" Weasel asked, inclining his head toward the big man.

Duvain's brow furrowed. "No. He's just—"

"Sure he is," Weasel persisted. "He's always off on his lonesome, or hangin' around you. I get that you two are brothers, but surely you're no better than the rest of us."

The statement surprised Duvain. "Better than you?"

Weasel took another mouthful of *ayrag*. "You keep your own company, spend every free moment hoverin' around each other, and he don't talk to the rest of us. Seems odd, is all. When it comes to battle, it's the bond between soldiers as keeps 'em alive."

Duvain's jaw dropped. This was the *last* thing he'd expected from any of them—Weasel most of all. The rat-faced Legionnaire had been the most vocal in his disgust after seeing Endyn's dragonskin. He'd been the one to pull the prank on Endyn.

"He..." Duvain took a deep breath. How could he explain that Endyn felt rejected, both because of his size—a deformity, according to

102

the Ministrants at the Sanctuary in Voramis—and the dragonskin? His words came out in a slow, hesitant voice. "He's not used to fitting in, I guess."

"Story of our lives, kid," Awr said. He took another long drink of wine. "Deadheads is for misfits and freaks." He indicated Weasel. "Bloodthirsty cunt." He thrust a finger at Owen. "Soldier afraid of blood." He indicated Rold and himself. "Career soldier and disgraced ex-convict."

Weasel shrugged. "Seems like fucked-up skin makes him right at home." He raised his voice to a shout. "Oi, big man!"

Endyn looked up.

"Yeah, you." Weasel waved him over. "No reason to be a stranger, now."

Endyn shot a glance at Duvain, who gave a tiny shrug. He'd wanted so much for the others to accept them, but he'd resigned himself to being an outsider. Endyn's happiness mattered more than his own— he'd made a promise to his mother to watch out for him. But if the rest of Squad Three was welcoming his brother…

Endyn stood with a groan and lumbered over.

"Here you go." Weasel handed him his half-full tankard. "I can't stand this stuff, so you might as well drink it."

Endyn hesitated. He'd grown wary of Weasel after the centipede prank.

"No trick," Weasel insisted. "Take it. After today, you earned it."

Endyn accepted and, bringing the tankard slowly to his lips, took a hesitant sip. After a moment, he downed the rest of the contents. That was the closest Weasel would come to an apology for his earlier remarks.

"Though I'd be *real* thorough checkin' your bedroll later," Weasel said to no one in particular. "I hear there's centipedes squirmin' around the longhouse."

Endyn voiced his anger with a growl and reached down for Weasel's collar. He lifted the little man physically from the ground and shook him like a dog shaking a rat.

"Take it easy!" Weasel cried. "Just a joke, I swear!"

Endyn held Weasel up to his face, fixing him with a furious glare. After a moment, a smile cracked his scowl. "Joke," he rumbled. "Good one."

Weasel's fear faded, replaced by disbelief. "You bastard!" he shrieked and lashed out with a half-hearted punch at Endyn's chest. The blow had as much effect as a mosquito pricking a bear. But when Endyn put him down, the little man was smiling.

Duvain's heart lightened. It was as close as the Legionnaires could come to acceptance. For someone who had been an outsider his whole life, it was more than enough.

Chapter Eight

Duvain couldn't help his fascination at the transformation that had gripped Saerheim. Colorful garlands festooned the longhouses, and the last autumn leaves had been carefully gathered and strewn over the ground of the main square like a carpet of red, yellow, and orange. The villagers of Saerheim wore their finest clothing, bright-hued tunics, breeches, vests, and cloaks dyed purple, green, and blue. A pair of musicians—the baker and blacksmith, oddly enough—sat at one corner of the square, filling the air with the sounds of pipe and drum.

Saerheim had become a lively place for *Heilirkvam,* the annual festival commemorating the midsummer. It was a celebration of a good year, an ode to summer and life, and a night to be filled with poetry, songs, and dancing.

Duvain understood little of what was being said, but he could certainly enjoy the bright colors of the festival. The smell of fresh-baked bread had permeated the village all day, and the rich, meaty scent of roasting pig, venison, and poultry hung thick around him. His stomach growled with anticipation of the feast.

He was fortunate: Squad Three would be off duty during the festivities. The Legionnaires of Squad Five had shot furious glares their way as they donned their polished armor and prepared for the night watch. The on-duty Legionnaires would be able to watch the ceremony only from the fringes as their patrol patterns permitted. But not too closely. Sergeant Brash had promised a flogging to any man caught away from his post. The sergeant wouldn't be attending the party, all the better to keep a sharp eye on his comrades.

A few of the night watch had tried to switch duties with them, especially Duvain, who had proven amenable to such bargains in the past. They'd offered him coins, liquor, trinkets, and other valuables—things he could have used, but which held no allure for him now. He wouldn't miss the celebration for anything.

Winter Festival in Northfield had been the *one* time of year he'd looked forward to. The little town had come alive with decorations, music, food, dancing, and laughter. People didn't stare at Endyn, for they were too busy having a good time to care. His brother had actually had a chance to step out and enjoy himself as well.

He checked his equipment one last time. He'd polished his armor to a bright sheen and buffed his boots until his hands ached. He had even taken pains to wash his extra tunic in the lake. He felt clean for the first time in weeks.

Endyn looked a fine sight in his armor. The brightness of Endyn's breastplate—crafted specially for him by a Legion armorer back in Voramis—outshone his own. A smile played on his big face. He enjoyed the Winter Festival as much as Duvain.

Owen and Rold had also paid extra attention to the state of their gear—they almost might have passed for respectable Legionnaires. Weasel, however, looked utterly miserable in his freshly polished armor. Opting for sleep rather than caring for his gear, he'd emerged from the roundhouse looking like he'd lost a battle with a muddy stick. Which had prompted a very angry, very loud lecture from Corporal Rold, and a stream of invective at the "dirty runt". Weasel had only *just* finished the thorough buffing of his breastplate after a full hour of listening to the corporal promise all manner of inventive disciplines—including digging for gold with nothing but his pencil-prick and running all the way back to Icespire in the buff—for disrespecting their squad.

The villagers of Saerheim had set out sawn tree trunks for chairs, arranging them in a broad circle around an empty space in the middle of the square. The clearing needed no boundary to outline it—the very stones themselves seemed to shine with an inner light. In the daylight, they appeared unremarkable, aside from their color: a black somehow darker than any onyx or obsidian he'd seen. But when the sun set, the stone seemed to reflect the flickering light of the torches and mirror the dark, starry sky high above.

Corporal Awr was already seated when they reached the square, face buried in a tankard. He hadn't lost his usual somber mien, but he seemed a bit less dour than usual. From beneath hooded brows, he watched the laughing, playing children, the women dressed in their colorful finery, and the men in their elegant furs and tunics.

"Corporal," Owen nodded and took a seat beside the man. Awr responded with a grunt.

"Is that more *ayrag*?" Weasel asked.

Awr nodded.

"Damn," Weasel groaned. He patted his stomach. "I've had the shits for two days now. That stuff don't sit well with me."

Awr shrugged and took another long swig of his drink.

One of the older men of Saerheim, a man who tilled the fields beside Cold Lake, approached with four large tankards. He said something in the Fehlan language; Duvain caught the words "welcome" and "night", but not much else.

Awr gave a two-word response and a nod, bringing a smile to the man's face. He held out the tankards for Weasel, Owen, Rold, and Duvain.

Endyn's brow furrowed, and a shadow passed across his face. Duvain could see his brother's mind working, his pain at being left out.

With a grin, the villager disappeared into a nearby longhouse. When he emerged a moment later, he carried a wooden vessel that was more cauldron than cup—easily half the size of a small barrel. Laughing, he presented it to Endyn and said something in the Fehlan tongue.

"Big cup for a big warrior, he says," Awr translated.

Endyn blushed, which only made the man's grin broader.

Duvain chuckled. "Look at that, Brother." He slapped Endyn's shoulder. "They like you."

Endyn bowed in thanks, and the Fehlan man responded in kind. Duvain waited for Awr to translate, but the corporal had his face buried in his mug.

"What did he say?" Endyn asked.

Duvain hesitated. "It sounded like he was saying 'thank you'. I think there was something about one of the houses in there, but I'm not sure."

"Oh." A grin broadened Endyn's huge face. He rumbled out a word that sounded like the Fehlan equivalent of "thank you". The villager laughed and gestured toward the hide containers that held the *ayrag.*

Endyn stood and went over to fill his massive bowl.

When his brother returned to his seat, Duvain cocked an eyebrow. "Since when have you been learning Fehlan?"

Endyn shrugged. "Listening to you and Awr."

"And why is he thanking *you*?" Duvain asked.

Endyn's face turned a bright pink. "I...helped them fix one of the houses," he rumbled.

Weasel snorted. "Held up the bloody roof single-handed, more like." He shook his head and gave a wicked grin. "Strong as an ox, your brother, even if he's almost as ugly."

Endyn said nothing, but took a long pull from his drinking bowl. When he wiped the line of *ayrag* from his mouth, a ghost of a smile remained.

A steady stream of Fehlans trickled into the square, until the open space was awash with laughing, talking, drinking men and women. Children darted among the adults, shouting and playing the sort of games youngsters enjoyed when the adults' backs were turned. Duvain counted close to two hundred people. Everyone in Saerheim had arrived for the festivities.

Someone produced a bone whistle, and soon a high-pitched tune drifted through the open square, adding to the refrain of the baker on the terracotta pipe and the blacksmith on his hide-skin drum. When the *tinkle* of bronze hand bells entered the fray, the celebration began in earnest.

The people of Saerheim certainly knew how to celebrate. Their dancing was like nothing Duvain had seen in Northfield. Men and women formed into two long lines facing each other. They followed the rhythm of the song with clapping hands, boots *clacking* against the stone of the square, keeping pace with their fellows. Back and forward they went, a combat of smiles, laughter, whirling skirts, and kicking feet.

Duvain, Endyn, and the other Legionnaires stomped and clapped in time with the music, adding their shouts and cries to the happy mix. For a few minutes, Duvain forgot where he was, but let himself be drawn into the marvelous new ceremony. He'd never experienced anything like it. These people led such simple lives, yet they celebrated that simplicity with such abandon. He was grinning like a fool and loving every minute of it.

Finally the music died down, and the breathless, laughing villagers surged toward the food and drink. The *ayrag* flowed freely, accompanied by mouth-watering food: roasted pork and goat, smoked fish, cooked grains, and the last autumn fruits and vegetables. The Fehlan language filled the square as two hundred people carried on a multitude of conversations.

No one invited the Legionnaires to join in. The villagers of Saerheim treated them with courtesy and served them along with the rest, but the language barrier caused a rift that could not be bridged. Awr, the only one who spoke the Fehlan tongue, refused to be drawn into any conversations. He remained hunched over his tankard, only moving to refill it when it was empty.

Duvain couldn't help watching the young women of Saerheim, with their long, flaxen tresses, pink cheeks, and strong features. Many of them rivaled even his height, a fact he found fascinating. He didn't try to strike up a conversation—he was too shy to talk to them, even in his own language—but found nothing wrong with simply observing them. They seemed aware of his eyes on them, and a few even looked his way with inviting smiles.

A tug on his sleeve snapped him around. Before him stood the young boy he'd seen hiding in Eira's skirts days before. He wore the colorful festive clothing like all the other children of Saerheim, and someone had clearly taken pains to scrub his face and hands, though his white-blond hair stuck out at wild angles.

With a broad smile, the boy rattled off a string of Fehlan words and held out a piece of bread. Duvain didn't need to understand the language to understand the gesture. When Duvain took the bread, the boy darted away. Duvain shouted a "thank you" after the fleeing child, who took refuge in the safety of his mother's skirts. His big blue eyes followed Duvain's movements as he broke the bread and stuffed a piece in his mouth. He exaggerated his enjoyment of the food, which elicited another shy smile.

One of the older men brought over a platter of food for them. Weasel and Rold dug in without a word, but Endyn and Duvain both used their limited Fehlan to offer their gratitude. The man smiled and gave them a polite nod before returning to the others. Owen sat in silence next to Awr, an odd expression—a mixture of longing and sorrow—on his face.

When Weasel noticed Owen's expression, he rolled his eyes. "Keeper's beard, Owen! Not this again."

Owen looked over to him and gave a sad shake of his head. "Can't help it. Issala would have loved this. The dancing, the singing, the celebration of life."

"*Of course* she would!" Weasel shook his head. "Awr here's the only one who hates a party."

Awr scowled but didn't rise to the bait.

"Look," Weasel said, "you're just goin' to make things worse if you keep thinkin' about it. You've still got two years left before you see her. Might as well make the most of the life you've got." A sly grin broadened his face, and his eyes went to the pretty brunette he'd been eyeing all night. "And let me tell you, life here ain't all that bad."

"Keep it in your pants, Weasel," Rold snapped. "Captain's orders."

Weasel's head snapped around, and his eyebrows rose. "You serious?"

Rold nodded. "Like a sword to the gut. Lord Virinus has already pissed off the natives enough for one lifetime—the man's no bloody diplomat, he's made that much clear, just a man rich enough to throw his influence and gold around to feel powerful. His treatment of the healer hasn't won him any allies. The last thing we need is someone getting in the family way and complaining to the captain."

A nasty smile spread Weasel's face. "Oh, there're plenty of means around that particular outcome."

Rold gripped Weasel's collar and yanked his face close. "Lay one finger on those girls, and Sarge has given me the thumbs up to slice your little prick off. Got it?"

Weasel scowled, but muttered, "Got it."

Rold looked at Duvain, Endyn, and Owen in turn. "Captain's made it crystal clear: enjoy the celebration, but keep your hands to yourselves. The Fehlans get mighty prickly when it comes to their daughters."

"Daughters are worth a fortune," Awr explained. "Fehlan fathers try to marry them off to the right men with a big enough dowry, set themselves up for life."

Duvain was disappointed, but he nodded. "Understood." Endyn nodded his comprehension as well.

"Good." Rold raised his tankard. "Then drink up and enjoy the party. Our watch doesn't roll around until dawn."

A drum beat sounded, and all eyes turned toward the cleared space in the center of the square. The blacksmith pounded on his hide

111

drums, the rhythm changing from festive to somber. The villagers quickly rushed to take their seats around the stage.

Elder Asmund strode into the cleared space and began to speak. The man's strong voice had a hypnotic rhythmic quality that reverberated across the square. Duvain found himself leaning forward to pay closer attention. Though he caught only an occasional word or phrase, he guessed it was a speech celebrating the end of the harvest or the arrival of winter.

Applause greeted the end of the speech, and Elder Asmund took a seat at the front of the crowd. All eyes turned toward the main longhouse.

Captain Lingram appeared in the doorway, dressed in his finest clothing, his armor polished to a brilliant sheen. A woman clung to his arm. She was beautiful, more beautiful than any of the other women in Saerheim. Her flaxen hair hung long and silky down to her waist, and she was tall—almost as tall as the captain—and lean. In her left hand, she gripped a stick that she swung across the ground, using it to navigate through the square.

The captain escorted the blind woman through the rows of seated villagers, helping her to step over the boundary logs and onto the stage. Her arm lingered for a moment on his before she released him.

"Now that ain't fair!" Weasel protested. "Why does he—?"

"Captain's prerogative," Rold cut him off with a sharp smile.

More than a few in the crowd caught it as well. Someone shouted something in the Fehlan tongue, eliciting an embarrassed smile from the captain. The blind woman answered in a sharp tone that brought laughter to the crowd, but there was no anger in her voice. The people of Saerheim clearly enjoyed this part of the spectacle.

One of the villagers placed a stringed instrument in her hands. The instrument resembled a harp, but with a hollow body that echoed and amplified the sound of the strings. When she strummed it, the strings resonated with a deep, throaty pitch that Duvain found alluring.

She started slowly, a rhythm that came quietly at first but grew in strength as each strum built upon the last. A tenuous sound, almost hesitant, yet holding the promise of growth. One of the hand bells joined her, adding into the building melody. When she opened her mouth and began to sing, Duvain was lost.

The words didn't matter—the music and her sonorous voice carried him along. From behind her, a willowy figure dressed in bright green scarves glided onto the stage. She was young and beautiful, graceful, with a supple body and fair skin. She danced to the tune of the music, her movements airy, playful, like a river sprite or fairy.

The rhythm of the music changed. From slow to chirpy and energetic, with a happy tone that brightened the light glowing stones and the torches ringing the stage. Another figure appeared on the stage, this one clad in bright yellow. Strong and confident, he twirled the young woman in his arms and lifted her high over his head. His power added to her grace, and her beauty enhanced his strength.

Duvain caught the word for "summer" among the lyrics of the song, and suddenly he understood. Spring and summer. Beauty and life.

The tune changed again, this time changing to a deeper, richer tone, melodious. It seemed the trees themselves bent toward the sound. The two dancers threw off their green and yellow clothing, revealing robes of orange and red beneath. The coming of autumn.

From behind the singer, another figure appeared. Elder Asmund, dressed in grey and white, with a long white cloak hanging from his shoulders. When he stepped onto the stage, the notes floating up from the lyre shifted lower. The drum added a quiet beat, which only increased the menace of the cloaked figure. Winter had come.

The man in grey and white stalked toward the dancing couple, who frolicked unaware of him. They twirled and spun, eyes locked on each other, faces radiant. Duvain found himself holding his breath as the white-robed man drew closer, reaching toward them with outstretched arm. He and the crowd sighed when the couple glided away at the last moment.

Winter pursued autumn. Though the colorful figures eluded their pursuer, the red and orange scarves hanging from their clothing fell with every step. The ground was soon littered with the bright-colored cloths. Beneath the scarves, the dancers wore dull brown robes. A bone pipe added its high-pitched wailing to the tune.

Melancholy mingled with despair in Duvain's chest. The music touched something deep inside him, and the lyrics and dance brought tears to his eyes. He knew the inevitable was coming: winter would triumph.

At last, the cloaked figure caught up to the two lovers, drawing them into the embrace of his white and grey robe. The young man and woman remained intertwined as they disappeared beneath the cloak, and the music fell to a quiet, mournful tune. A few final notes of the pipe, and it fell silent. The drum and hand bells faded into the night. Only the strumming lyre remained, accompanied by the haunting sound of the woman's singing.

Finally, her voice trailed off, leaving the lyre to carry them to the end. Yet, in those last moments, the tune changed again. The song remained deep and forlorn, yet here and there a few of the bright, cheery notes were sprinkled in. From beneath one corner of the white and grey robe, a green-gloved hand appeared.

Silence.

Thunderous applause broke from the crowd, and the people rose to their feet. With a broad grin, Elder Asmund lifted his cloak and helped the two dancers to stand. They swept a bow, which brought fresh cheers. The three of them supported the blind woman as the crowd shouted and whistled their approval. Though she blushed, a broad smile spread across her face.

Duvain found himself at a loss for words. Judging by the expressions of the others beside him, they felt something similar. Endyn brushed a tear from his cheek, and Owen swallowed hard. Weasel buried his face in his mug.

Oddly enough, Awr was smiling—an expression Duvain had never seen before.

"Always loved that," the grizzled man rasped. He spoke to no one in particular. "She's better than anyone I've seen in *Storbjarg*."

Duvain's eyebrows rose. Storbjarg was the largest Fehlan village—a city, really—home to the chieftain of the *Fjall* clan. When had Awr been among the *Fjall*?

Before Duvain could say anything, an enraged shout echoed across the square. He whirled toward the source of the sound: Lord Virinus' hut. The nobleman himself was striding toward the village square, dragging a struggling Eira in his wake.

"Legionnaires, to me!" the nobleman shouted.

Whether entranced by the song or shocked by the fury in Lord Virinus' voice, none of the Legionnaires moved.

"To me!" the nobleman cried again. He dragged the ancient healer through the crowd and onto the stage, where he hurled her to the bluestone courtyard.

Captain Lingram stepped onto the stage. "What is the meaning of this, Lord Virinus?" he demanded.

Lord Virinus' face was twisted in a mask of rage. "Captain Lingram, I demand you execute this witch at once!"

Chapter Nine

The villagers were on their feet in an instant. Angry shouts echoed from the crowd, and a couple of men surged toward the old woman to help her up to her feet.

"Captain Lingram," Lord Virinus snapped, "I have given you a command."

"I heard you, my lord." Captain Lingram's face could have been made from flint, so hard was his expression. "But I don't believe I understood."

"What's not to understand?" Lord Virinus thrust a finger at the healer. "That witch went against my instructions and administered more of her foul concoctions to my guest. As a noble of Icespire and the Prince's Envoy, I am in charge of this outpost—*pathetic* as it may be— and fully within my rights to have her executed."

"My lord," Captain Lingram protested, "this is no outpost. This is a village. *Their* village."

"Were Duke Dyrund here, you would obey him without question!" Lord Virinus' eyes flashed. "As his successor and the one entrusted with carrying out his final mission, that authority falls to me!"

"Be that as it may," Captain Lingram gave a dismissive wave, "surely you cannot expect me to execute her. She was doing her duty— she is Saerheim's healer, after all."

"And if that duty leads to the death of my charge?" Lord Virinus demanded. "By then, it will be too late—not only for the innocent girl who lies ill, but for our alliance with the *Fjall*."

The name of the clan, well known to all Fehlans, brought a gasp from the crowd. The villagers muttered amongst themselves, shooting glances at the hut Lord Virinus had claimed for his own.

A hand gripped Duvain's shoulder. "Move, now," Awr rasped in his ear.

Duvain shot the corporal a look. "What are we doing?" he asked from the corner of his mouth.

"Supporting our captain." Awr's face had gone cold, dead, but fury burned in his eyes. "Just in case he needs us." His hand rested on the hilt of his sword.

Slowly, Duvain stood, trying hard not to jangle his armor. He followed Awr and Rold as they slipped through the crowd. A few of the villagers they moved aside shot them angry glares, but their expressions changed as Awr muttered a few words in Fehlan. Some of the men of Saerheim broke from the crowd and hurried toward their homes.

Duvain's gut clenched. This could get ugly very quickly.

"My lord, I fully understand how important the girl's life is. Indeed, important enough that I and my entire company of men have been sent to safeguard her." Captain Lingram gestured to the healer. "But Eira was only trying to help. Duke Dyrund would—"

"The Duke is dead!" Lord Virinus shouted. "Taken by the same Wraithfever that even now ravages the girl. The same fever that would destroy all we've worked so hard for."

The old woman held up a wooden bowl and rattled off a stream of angry words in Fehlan. Captain Lingram listened, then turned back to the nobleman.

"She says the fever is about to break, but only if you allow her to help." He pointed to the bowl. "That poultice should bring her temperature down and restore her to consciousness. By tomorrow, she would be able to eat solid food."

The old woman continued speaking, and Captain Lingram translated. "She has seen the Wraithfever before—the Wasting Decay, she calls it. It is a stubborn illness, one that weakens the body until it can no longer fight for itself. If you keep her away from the girl, she will die."

Lord Virinus' lips twisted into a sneer. "Of *course* she'd say that! She would say anything to save her life."

Captain Lingram spoke in a quiet voice. "I believe her."

The nobleman's eyebrows rose. "You'd take the word of a savage?"

"Not a savage, my lord. A *Fehlan*. One of our allies."

The sneer returned to Lord Virinus' face.

"They may lead simple lives, my lord," Captain Lingram said, "but there is wisdom in their ways. Their healers may not live in temples or wear shining white robes. But I've seen what they can do."

The captain shot a glance at Awr. "They have brought men back from the brink of death. When I lay dying from my wounds, they did the impossible. I only stand here today because of them." He looked at Endyn. "But more importantly, they have shown us compassion when they have only reason to resent us." He thrust a finger at the old healer. "I have watched her provide comfort and relief to my men since our arrival. She has done nothing but help. So *yes*, my lord. I *will* take her word when she says that she believes she can cure the fever. Only a *fool* would ignore advice from one so experienced."

Lord Virinus recoiled as if slapped. "You call me a fool, Captain? Insulting your superiors is—"

"I gave no insult." Captain Lingram shook his head. "I simply made a statement; whether you choose to embody that fool or not is entirely your decision."

Lord Virinus took a step closer. "And if I choose to force the matter?" There was no mistaking the menace in his voice.

119

"I would entreat you to reconsider, my lord." Captain Lingram said, simply. "You fear the repercussions of what would happen if Eirik Throrsson's daughter dies, and rightly so. But what will happen when the other tribes discover you executed their healer? One of the most revered among *all* the clans?"

"Nothing!" Lord Virinus spat. "They are our subjects."

"Allies," Captain Lingram corrected.

"Vassals!" The nobleman's voice rose to a shout. "They pledged their loyalty to the Prince long ago." He gestured around. "Why else do you think we can simply march into their village and *demand* they house us?"

Captain Lingram shook his head. "My lord, if you order her execution, you will doom the alliance between Icespire and the *Fjall*. Perhaps *all* the clans."

"Nonsense." The nobleman snorted. "They will do nothing, because we are the only thing standing between them and the Eirdkilrs." He raised his voice so *all* the Legionnaires around him could hear. "That's right, the Eirdkilrs have sworn to exterminate any Fehlan who aid us in our war. They have attacked the *Eyrr* and decimated the *Fjall* warband. Why else do you think the *Hilmir* himself was so willing to talk peace? We are their only hope of survival."

He turned his attention back to Captain Lingram, and spoke in a low, menacing voice. "We are their only hope."

By now, Awr had maneuvered into position behind Captain Lingram. At his command, Duvain, Endyn, and the others of Squad Three spread out. They'd keep the angry villagers back, give Captain Lingram time to control the situation. The look in Awr's eyes spoke clearly: if it came down to it, they'd be ready to jump to Captain Lingram's orders.

"But what happens when we become *worse* than the monsters they fear, Lord Virinus?" The captain's tone matched the nobleman's, but filled with ice and steel. "That is how revolts begin."

"Revolts that are always crushed." Lord Virinus shook a clenched fist. "They cannot hope to survive against us."

"With the Eirdkilrs on one side and the rest of Fehl at our backs, what are our chances then?"

Lord Virinus' face creased into a scowl. "What do you know of such things, *Captain*?" He spoke the last word as an insult. "I learned diplomacy at the feet of Duke Dyrund himself. But, you, you are just a soldier, not accustomed to the ways of politics."

"Perhaps," Captain Lingram admitted, inclining his head, "but I've spent enough time among the Fehlans to know that this will not end well."

"We'll see about that," Lord Virinus snapped.

Duvain had been watching Lord Virinus so intently that he'd failed to notice the four men moving into position behind the nobleman. The mercenaries were no-nonsense, hard men with wary eyes. Their hands hovered near their sword hilts as they watched their lord.

"Be ready," Awr rumbled.

"Corporal, this is madness!" Owen whispered. "Surely you can't expect us to—"

"Lord Virinus, I will say it one last time: *please* reconsider your orders." Captain Lingram's tone turned pleading. "This will only end badly."

Lord Virinus' jaw set into a stubborn line. "Captain Lingram, I am giving you a direct command." He thrust a finger toward the healer. "You are to carry out her execution immediately."

Though only a few villagers spoke the Princelander tongue, clearly they understood the nobleman's words. Hand axes, scythes, and even a few old swords sprouted in Fehlan hands, and a line of men formed between Eira and the nobleman.

"Captain, you have your orders," Lord Virinus shouted.

"No." The single word, spoken with such determination, rocked Lord Virinus to the core.

"What?" The nobleman demanded. "You refuse to carry out a command from the Duke's hand-picked successor?"

"*This* command, I do." Captain Lingram's voice remained calm, but his back was rigid, his shoulders tense.

"You bastard!" Lord Virinus' sneer transformed into a vicious smile. "You've finally done it. You've finally given me an excuse to have you court-martialed." He waved at the Legionnaires in the crowd. "I've dozens of witnesses who saw you refuse a direct order. Your days in the Legion are *finished.*"

"I didn't see anything of the sort," Awr rasped. He turned to Duvain. "Did you?"

After a moment of hesitation, Duvain shook his head. "No, Corporal!"

Awr turned to Endyn and Owen. "In fact, none of us did, did we, lads?"

"Sorry, Corporal!" Weasel replied. "Had a bit too much of the *ayrag*! Damned alcohol's messin' with my eyesight. I couldn't tell you if I was lookin' at a man or a horse's ass."

Lord Virinus' eyes went wide, and his expression grew enraged. "Why you little hedge-born pissant!" He spoke through clenched teeth. "I'll have your head for that. All of your heads!"

Captain Lingram shot a disapproving glare at Awr and the rest of them. "Enough of this, Virinus. If you intend to have me court-martialed when we return to Icespire, so be it. I will hold my head high and give testimony in the Swordsman's Court."

"When they hear that you disobeyed a direct command—" Lord Virinus began.

"My orders from Commander Galerius were to keep you safe until the Duke's rider arrives with the Wraithfever cure and the *Hilmir's* daughter is well enough to travel." He dropped his voice. "And I fully intend to protect you, even if that means from yourself."

The nobleman's face grew livid. "And there he is: Lingram the Bold. Lingram the Hero." Disgust twisted his face. "You think you're better than me because you earned some ridiculous nom de guerre for fighting. Any lowborn whorespawn can fight and die. And that's exactly what you are, what you've always been. I saw it in your eyes even when we were boys running around my father's estate. You resented the fact that you were the stable boy and I the lord's son. You've always been jealous of me, and now you get your moment to take it out on me." He spread his arms wide. "Congratulations, Lingram. You've won."

The captain shook his head. "I never hated you, Myron. If anything, I admired you. You and your father both. I wanted to be like you. It drove me to join the Legion so I could earn a name you both would be proud of."

This revelation hit Lord Virinus like a blow to the gut.

"But the boy I knew became the man that stands before me." Captain Lingram gave a sad shake of his head. "A man driven by pettiness, greed, and a desire for power. That is not a man I admire."

"So you turn against me?" Lord Virinus took a step closer, his four mercenaries at his heels. "You defy me in public, humiliate me, then do it again in front of your own Legion?"

"Get ready," Awr muttered.

A small gesture from Captain Lingram held them at bay. "I did not mean to humiliate you, Myron. I simply could not stand by while you raised a hand against a man who deserved better than to swing from a hangman's rope. Just as I will not stand by now."

"A decision that will be your last!" Lord Virinus shouted. "Your career in the Legion is *over!* By this time next week, you will be swinging at the end of a hangman's noose."

Captain Lingram raised his head. "Then I will accept my fate, as I always have, knowing I died doing as your father taught me to: the right thing."

Lord Virinus' face turned white, and a look of mixed outrage and shame burned in his eyes.

Duvain tensed, hand on his sword hilt. The mercenaries behind Lord Virinus had already half-drawn their swords. Squad Three had the odds on their side, but once blood was spilled, there was no going back.

He glanced up at Endyn. His brother's eyes were firmly fixed on the mercenaries, his massive jaw set. He knew what he had to do.

A blood-curdling scream shattered the tense silence.

Chapter Ten

Duvain whirled toward the sound. It had come from the east gate!

Another scream, followed by the clash of steel. A moment later, the trumpeting blare of Squad Five's cornum echoed in the night.

"We're under attack!" Rold cried.

Awr was already sprinting toward the gate, sword in hand, with Owen, Weasel, and Rold a step behind him.

Duvain's feet refused to move.

"Let's go!" Endyn shouted.

Duvain stared up at his brother. His mind screamed at him to move, but his body failed to cooperate.

Captain Lingram's voice pierced the buzzing in his head. "Get to the east gate, now, and send reinforcements to the west gate to cover our rear!"

"Aye, Captain!" shouted one of the other off-duty Legionnaires.

A strong hand gripped Duvain's arm and dragged him after the rest of his company. After a moment, he found his own feet and ran without Endyn's help. Somehow, in the confusion, he'd managed to retain his grip on his sword.

Chaos reigned at the east gate. Four Legionnaires fought two dark, hulking figures, while a fifth Legionnaire raced toward the two huge men struggling to lift the gate's locking bar. The Legionnaire cut one down, only to be crushed by the huge bar, swung by the second fur-clad barbarian. The man howled and yanked the gate open. A heartbeat too late, a thrown hand axe silenced his cries.

Dark figures spilled from the shadows, rushing toward the open gate without a sound. Somehow, the absence of noise was even more ominous. The foremost figures burst through the gate and engaged the Legionnaires rushing to meet them. They were huge—nearly as tall and broad as Endyn—wearing huge pelts slung over their back. One of the Legionnaires hacked at the back of one enemy, only for his sword to bounce off the pelt. The barbarian whirled, swinging his huge axe, and the Legionnaire's head rolled free.

Two of the gate guards had fallen, but the alarm had been raised. Dozens more Legionnaires rushed from their patrols, streaming toward the skirmish before the open gates.

Awr reached the battle well ahead of them. A furious cry burst from his lips as he hacked at the nearest barbarian. The shaggy-haired man turned the blow aside with his axe, but Awr followed it up with a chop that nearly took off the man's leg. Awr's sword took the fallen savage in the throat.

"Form up!" he shouted. His rasping voice echoed even above the din of battle. "Form ranks now!"

Duvain's training kicked in. He raced toward the shield wall forming just inside the gate. He took his place in the third rank, just next to Endyn.

Horror raced through him as he realized he'd left his shield in his quarters. Captain Lingram had insisted on the Legionnaires wearing full armor at all times, but he'd left his heavy shield and long spear behind for the celebration. He had only his short sword to face the onrushing threat.

"Forward, march! Double time." At the corporal's command, the line began a steady jog toward the enemy. The foremost two ranks had their shields, and the rest of Squad Four joined the third rank. Their swords would only serve if an enemy broke through the line.

The barbarians saw them coming, and raised their voices in an animal howl. Shaking their massive weapons—axes, spears, and spiked wooden clubs—they charged.

"Damn, damn, damn, damn!" Someone in the line was cursing at a steady volume. Duvain realized it was him. A fist of iron clenched his heart, and panic tugged at the back of his mind. He had no time to think before the wave of barbarians crashed into their shield wall.

The impact drove the foremost ranks a step backward. The man before him slammed into him, nearly knocking the breath from his lungs. Sergeant Brash's training asserted itself and Duvain caught the man and shoved him forward. The shield wall held.

The barbarians swung their massive weapons in powerful arcs, but they clanged off the iron rims or crunched into the wooden faces of the Legion shields. Men cried out beneath the impact. One Legionnaire dropped his shield, and a barbarian spear disemboweled him.

But the Legion had teeth of its own. The short swords of the foremost rank struck low, aiming for legs and abdomens. The stabbing, slicing blades made quick work of the huge figures pressing against the shield wall. At the corporal's shouted command—Duvain's mind hardly registered the words, but his body reacted—the ranks shoved forward, driving the barbarians back. They stumbled from the impact, only to recover and hurl themselves at the shield wall again.

The clash of battle and the screams of dying men filled Duvain's world. The stink of blood, mud, and loosening bowels flooded his nostrils, accompanied by the reek of his own terrified sweat. A hand on his back kept him moving forward, pressing him toward the enemy no matter how much his mind shrieked at him to flee. Endyn's presence at his side was the only thing keeping him grounded in the midst of such chaos and terror.

Suddenly, there was silence. The last barbarian fell beneath a stabbing short sword, and a heavy boot crushed his throat. The pounding of Duvain's pulse in his ears drowned out everything.

"Meat?" A hand shook his arm. "Meat, you hurt?"

Rold's face hovered in his vision. Duvain blinked and tried to speak. His mouth refused to form words.

Rold slapped his face; the pain barely registered. "Snap out of it! You've got to move."

"Duvain." The rumbling voice—Endyn's, a dim part of his mind registered—drew him back to reality. "Duvain."

He drew in a shuddering breath, gasping, and staggered. Blinking hard, he wiped the torrent of sweat from his eyes.

"Welcome back, meat." Rold said. The harsh anger had gone, replaced by a congeniality terribly at odds with the corporal's usual demeanor. "You survived your first shield wall. We'll celebrate later— there's work to do. Find a shield and spear and arm up."

Duvain scanned the area. Bodies lay on the ground—close to a dozen Legionnaires and at least as many of the white fur-clad barbarians. Blood, so much blood, turned the earth to mud. The metallic tang rose into his nostrils. He wanted to retch, wanted to empty his stomach at the scene of carnage, but Rold's insistent voice kept him moving. "Now, meat! There may be more of them."

He turned to stumble back to his quarters, but Rold snagged his arm and shoved him toward the corpses. "Get one of theirs. Keeper knows they won't need it!"

Duvain stooped and fumbled for a fallen spear. Blood stained its edge and soaked into the wooden haft. When he lifted it, he found himself with two cracked halves. He stared down at the fallen soldier— the same axe that shattered the spear had split open his skull.

He tugged the shield free of the soldier's lifeless fingers. The fallen Legionnaire gave up his protection without a protest. Duvain turned and stumbled over another prone figure. This body had once been a barbarian. His flesh was stained an odd blue color—similar in shade to the festive robes of the Fehlans—but he had the same long, blond hair, strong features, and heavy beard of the villagers of Saerheim.

Yet there was an oddly bestial quality to his features. Even in death, he appeared more monster than man.

"Watcher's twisted taint!" Weasel's voice echoed from a short distance away. The rat-faced Legionnaire was crouched over a fallen body, knife in one hand and the corpse's ear in the other. "It's the bleedin' Eirdkilrs, ain't it?"

The word turned Duvain's blood to ice.

Awr, standing over him, nodded. "Damned right it is." His face twisted into a frown. "What the *bloody* hell are they doing this far north?" He lifted his eyes to the east. "Front lines are a long way off. Raiding party, maybe?"

With a savage cut, Weasel sliced the barbarian's ear free. "Judgin' by the number, has to be." His voice held a note of desperation—he *truly* wanted to believe it.

"Corporal Awr, report!" Captain Lingram's voice sounded cool, confident even amidst the carnage.

Awr snapped a salute. "Four dead, Captain. Eight wounded, two seriously."

"Get the wounded to the main longhouse for Eira to tend to them. Haul the dead off to the side—Eirdkilrs in one pile, ours in another."

"So they *are* the Eirdkilrs, Captain?" Owen asked. He'd come up behind Weasel on Captain Lingram's heels. Blood trickled from a wound in his forehead. He looked queasy, and vomit stained the corners of his mouth, but he'd gotten his hands on a spear and shield.

"Much as I hate to say it, that's them, no doubt about it." Captain Lingram crouched over the body. "Their size alone would be a dead giveaway. Add to that the war paint and these furs—they come from a Wasteland ice bear—and there's only one clan they could be."

"Keeper's horny elbows!" Awr breathed.

"Where are my scouts?" Captain Lingram demanded of Sergeant Brash, who stood a short distance away tending to a wounded soldier.

Sergeant Brash shook his head. "They went out earlier, haven't gotten back." He pressed a cloth against the Legionnaire's shoulder, trying to stanch the flow of blood from a deep gash.

"Damn!" Captain Lingram's forehead furrowed—the first sign of worry Duvain had seen. He pondered a moment before speaking. "All companies, arm up and get to the gates. Double the watches, and keep patrols along those lines. If there are more of them out there, I want to know *before* they hit us. Got it?"

"Aye, Captain!" Sergeant Brash said.

Squad One, already clad in full armor, rushed toward the gate, which someone—in all the confusion, Duvain didn't know who—had had the good sense to close. The Legionnaires mounted the parapets and stared out into the darkness. There was no mistaking the sudden nervous tension that permeated the entire village.

"Squad Three, grab your weapons and get back here. Double time." Sergeant Brash ordered.

"Sir!" Weasel saluted—every trace of his usual mockery gone, all professional soldier now—and sprinted toward their quarters in the main longhouse. Duvain, Endyn, and the rest of the company followed. Duvain's legs felt leaden, his feet numb. But the sight of Endyn stumbling ahead of him forced him to keep up. He couldn't let his brother face this threat alone.

Entering the longhouse felt like stepping into a hell of blood and pain. The eight wounded had been dragged here to be tended by Eira. The old woman knelt over one soldier, using a needle and thread to stitch up a gaping tear in his shoulder. She barked out commands in Fehlan, and two young women rushed to obey her orders.

"I bet Lord Virinus sure is glad he didn't have her executed now," Weasel muttered.

The cries and groans of the wounded men followed Duvain through the longhouse. His shield and spear remained where he'd left them resting against the wall. Seizing them, he rushed back toward the exit. He couldn't help glancing down at the still, pale figure lying on the ground. The man had succumbed to the gaping wound in his abdomen, where an Eirdkilr axe had hacked through his mail shirt, just below his breastplate. He'd died a painful death.

The night seemed suddenly chilly when Duvain emerged from the longhouse. He sprinted to catch up with Endyn and Weasel, who raced toward the gate at full speed. The clanking of their armor sounded oddly quiet beneath the hum of the village. Most of the people remained gathered in the main square, talking in low voices. Their faces were grim. They knew why the Eirdkilrs had come.

Of Lord Virinus, there was no sign. His four mercenaries stood at the entrance to their little hut, swords drawn and faces serious. If they were afraid, they showed no sign.

Duvain could only imagine what his face looked like. He was terrified, no doubt about it. Only the shouted orders of Rold, Awr, and Sergeant Brash kept him moving.

The tension among the men around the gate had grown so thick it almost stifled him. They felt just as he did, as unprepared and fearful as he. Only the few Legionnaires who had served under Captain Lingram showed no sign of fear.

"Orders, Captain?" Sergeant Brash was asking.

"Gates fortified, patrols moving?" Captain Lingram asked.

"Aye." The sergeant nodded. "No one's getting within pissing range of us before we see them."

Captain Lingram rubbed his chin. "If we had scouts, we might be able to get a better view of what's going on out there. But I don't want to risk anyone else getting lost or caught by surprise."

"So what do you suggest?" the sergeant asked.

Captain Lingram ground his teeth. "We hold. Get the villagers buttoned up in the longhouses, and keep a sharp eye on the surrounding forest, lakeside, and farms. Any movement, you sound the alarm."

"Aye, Captain!" Sergeant Brash saluted.

"Captain Lingram!" A nasal, pompous voice sounded from behind the captain.

The captain's jaw worked, but his voice was calm as he turned. "Yes, Lord Virinus?"

"I demand a situation report at once." The words were spoken in the petulant tone of a toddler.

"Eirdkilr raiders, a small detachment, by all appearances. The scouts haven't returned, so there's no way of knowing what's out there."

The nobleman blanched, his eyes filled with fear. "And what do you intend to do, Captain?" he demanded.

Captain Lingram replied. "Sit tight. Keep watch. If there are more of them, prepare ourselves for a fight."

"How?" Lord Virinus breathed as he crouched over a dead barbarian. "How in the Keeper's name have they gotten so far?"

Captain Lingram shrugged. "My guess is that this party managed to skirt the main force. They either stumbled across the village and decided to raid, or…" He trailed off.

"Or what, Captain?" Lord Virinus insisted.

"Or somehow they knew you were here." The words were spoken so quietly Duvain nearly missed them.

Lord Virinus' eyebrows shot up. "Impossible! Our mission was kept absolutely confidential. Only the highest-ranked members of the Icespire court knew of the Duke's task."

"But there's a chance someone from the *Fjall* camp leaked the information, isn't there?" Captain Lingram asked.

After a moment, Lord Virinus inclined his head. "The possibility does exist."

"Then we have to assume the Eirdkilrs know why you're here, and that they're coming for the girl." The captain pointed to Lord Virinus' hut. "We also have to assume there are more out there—how many, I don't know, but the Eirdkilrs wouldn't send such a small detachment for such an important task. Which means you have to make plans to depart *immediately* for Sentry Garrison."

Lord Virinus shook his head. "Absolutely not! The *Hilmir's* daughter is too weak to—"

Captain Lingram's jaw clenched. "At this point, my lord, I believe there is a greater risk to her life if you stay here. The Eirdkilrs know you're here, so here is where they'll be coming. My men can hold them off, give you a chance to cover some serious ground."

"No." Lord Virinus crossed his arms. "Branda's fever hasn't broken, and she hasn't eaten in days. Such a hasty flight would kill her."

"And so will the Eirdkilrs. At least if you flee, there's a chance she'll live long enough to recover." Captain Lingram spoke in a firm voice. "I *strongly* suggest you heed my advice and prepare to depart."

Lord Virinus gave a dismissive wave. "I will take your advice under consideration, Captain, but for now we stay put."

Captain Lingram drew a deep breath through his nostrils, but nodded. "Of course, my lord. Now, if you will excuse me—"

"Rider from the southeast!" the cry cut off his words.

Captain Lingram whirled. The cry had come from one of the Legionnaires on the wall. He raced toward the gate and rushed onto the rampart. "Where?"

The soldier pointed off into the distance. "There!"

From his position in the line, Duvain couldn't see the rider. His gut tensed. Were they about to be under attack again? He tightened his grip on his spear and wiped his sweaty shield hand on his pants.

The pounding of hooves grew louder, and a shout echoed from beyond the walls.

"Open the gates!" Captain Lingram commanded.

Two soldiers rushed to the gate, lifted the bar, and swung one of the doors open. A rider pounded through the opening. His horse's hooves kicked up crimson mud as he drew to a halt in the courtyard.

"Where's the commanding officer?" the man shouted. It *wasn't* one of the two scouts that had gone out earlier.

"Here!" Captain Lingram shouted. Lord Virinus' echoed "I am!" came a moment later.

The rider glanced between the two men, then strode toward Captain Lingram. "Captain Lingram, sir, I've a message for you from Commander Galerius."

"Hand it over." The captain held out a hand.

The messenger drew a parchment from his satchel and pressed it into the captain's hand. "I'm sorry I couldn't bring better news." He suddenly deflated, as if relieved of an enormous weight. He staggered and would have fallen if not for Sergeant Brash's strong arm.

Captain Lingram unfolded the parchment and scanned its contents. His face grew ashen. The sight of their unflappable captain afraid filled Duvain with a gut-twisting dread.

"Thank you, soldier," Captain Lingram said in a quiet voice. "Get yourself to the longhouse for some food and rest."

"Aye, sir." The rider saluted. "Been riding hard since yesterday afternoon. It'd be good to get some warm food in me."

"Go," the captain told him. "But if this message is true, we'll have need of you soon."

With a salute, the messenger strode toward the main longhouse.

Captain Lingram spoke before Lord Virinus. "My lord, you need to see this."

The nobleman snatched the parchment from his hands. As he read, his face went from florid to pale to a sickening shade of grey. "By the Swordsman!" he breathed. "It can't be."

Captain Lingram's expression grew somber. "We have to assume it is. The question, *sir*, is what you want to do now."

Lord Virinus' mouth hung open, and he stared at the captain with unseeing eyes. "What...I...want to...do?" he mumbled, as if dumbstruck.

"Yes, my lord," the captain said. "As the Duke's successor, you have a choice to make. Do we hold our position and hope we can stand against *that?*" He thrust a finger at the note. "Or do we flee?"

Lord Virinus' lips worked soundlessly. All his pompous arrogance had fled, replaced by hesitance. Dangerous in such a perilous situation. "I-I..." He swallowed.

"My suggestion, my lord," the captain said, "is flight. The walls will only hold for so long. If we can get out before they reach us, we've a chance of reaching safety. Or at least enough of us escaping to get you back to Sentry Garrison with the girl alive, hopefully long enough for the Duke's rider to bring the Wraithfever cure. Right now, that's *all* that matters."

Lord Virinus stared at the captain, agog. He seemed at a loss for words.

"My lord, you need to make a decision *now!*" Captain Lingram snapped. "Our lives are all in your hands. Either take command, or step aside so I can do my job." He fixed the nobleman with a baleful glare. "The choice is yours."

Lord Virinus' face went even paler.

Captain Lingram nodded. "So be it." He raised his voice so all could hear. "Deadheads, as of this moment, Lord Virinus has ceded command to me, and I am in charge until such a time as we reach safety. Is that understood?"

"Yes, Captain!" the Legionnaires echoed.

Captain Lingram turned his back on the dumbstruck nobleman and strode toward the men gathered before the gate. He held the parchment high. "I have just received a message from Commander Galerius. Our army defeated the Eirdkilrs at Hangman's Hill, but the enemy withdrew before they could be routed, and now they are roaming the northern Fjall and southern Deid lands, razing friendly villages and slaughtering our allies. The general sent us warning to be aware, but I believe the Eirdkilrs are coming directly here."

He thrust a finger at Lord Virinus. "The girl accompanying Lord Virinus is the daughter of Eirik Throrsson, and the Eirdkilrs know what will happen should our alliance with *Fjall* be cemented. There is no doubt in my mind that they are coming here to kill her. If she dies, so too dies our hope of peace in Fehl."

The captain looked from soldier to soldier. "But the Eirdkilrs didn't count on one thing: us. They failed to account for the Deadheads that stood between them and their prize. I say we make them pay for that mistake. What say you?"

"Hoo-rah!" Corporal Awr shouted. The other veterans echoed the shout, and a few of the older Deadheads echoed it as well.

"They call this company Deadheads because they believe you are the dregs of the Legion of Heroes. So be it!" The captain smiled. "Let them call us what they will. Let us wear the name with pride, and let us make it a name that every Eirdkilr bastard remembers. For it will be the name of the brave Legionnaires that spit in their faces when others cowered!"

"Hoo-rah!" More voices took up the cry.

"We cannot stand before the Eirdkilrs—according to Commander Galerius, they number at least five hundred."

"Now four hundred and some, Captain!" Weasel shouted.

"Right you are, soldier." Captain Lingram nudged one of the barbarian corpses with a boot. "We've proven that our shields, swords, and spears are as deadly as any of the other companies in the Legion. We've already shown that we can stand our ground and face the barbarians head on. But now it's time for us to prove that we can think with these dead heads of ours."

Laughter rippled among the ranks.

Captain Lingram grinned. "The walls of Saerheim are strong, and the cliffs provide us cover to the south and north, guard our retreat. But we are too few to hold off five hundred—"

"Four hundred and some!" Weasel chanted.

"—Eirdkilrs," Captain Lingram continued without pause. "We have a duty to protect the people of Saerheim, and a duty to protect Lord Virinus and Throrsson's daughter. If we stand and fight, we fail in those duties. If we retreat, we have a chance of survival. Though it goes against everything I have learned as a Legionnaire, I value my life over my pride or a chance at glory. We run, Deadheads. We run to fight another day, fight to the last man in order to protect those given into our charge. What say you?"

"Hoo-rah!" Every voice in the line echoed the cry now.

"Sergeant Brash!" Captain Lingram called.

"Yes, Captain!" Brash said.

Captain Lingram pointed to the south gate. "I expect the enemy to come from that way. Cold Lake and the cliffs give us cover enough that they can't come from west, and I doubt the Eirdkilrs have had time to go the long way around to the north. That means *this* is their only way in. Keep the walls manned until the last minute, but be prepared to pull out when I sound the alarm."

"Understood, Captain." The sergeant saluted.

"Sergeant Danver, have Squad Four prepare the villagers to leave immediately."

The sergeant named saluted. "Aye, sir." He snapped his fingers, and the men of his squad fell out of line and raced toward the city square.

Captain Lingram strode after them. "I will explain everything to the villagers for you, and will translate…" His voice faded as the distance grew.

"Squad Three, Squad One, onto the wall!" Sergeant Brash shouted.

Duvain, Endyn, and the others raced up to the ramparts. They crowded in beside the men already in position, jostling to get a good view. The pointed tips of the wooden palisade wall ended just below Duvain's neck level. Endyn's head, shoulders, and chest protruded well above the protective cover.

"Meat shield!" Rold called. "Get down to the gate, now."

Endyn shot a curious glance at Duvain, then at the corporal. "Sir?" he rumbled.

"Much as I'd love for the Eirdkilrs to send all their arrows at that pretty head of yours," Corporal Rold said, "a strong man like you'd come in handy keeping that gate closed in case the bastards decide to bring a battering ram."

Endyn nodded. "Yes, Corporal!"

Duvain gripped his forearm. "Be safe, Brother."

"You, too." With a nod, Endyn lumbered down the steps. He strode to the gate, where he stood waiting, shield and massive hewing spear gripped in his huge hand.

A tense silence descended on the ramparts. The camp behind them was abuzz with activity, but the only sound on the ramparts was the clanking of armor or the nervous coughing of the Legionnaires. All eyes fixed on the forest and lake. They knew what lay out there—all that remained was to wait.

Long minutes passed without movement. The wind no longer whispered across the lake, and it seemed the leaves had ceased their rustling. Utter stillness, an absence of sound that felt terrifying. Duvain's heart hammered against his ribs.

A light appeared across the lake. Little more than a pinprick, so small it had to be far away. Another appeared beside it, then another, and still more. Golden lights appeared in the darkness, skirting the lake, dancing through the forest like will-o-the-wisps, growing larger with every passing second. Duvain lost count after thirty, and still they continued to multiply. The lights outnumbered the stars twinkling in the sky.

They drew closer, growing until Duvain could make out the massive figures of men carrying torches. The shores of Cold Lake stood a mere three hundred paces from the east gate, and the huge barbarians covered the ground in loping strides. Their shaggy ice bear furs gave them a bestial appearance, like monsters from the stories his father had told him and Endyn to terrify them.

But they were *very* real.

The call of a horn shattered the tense silence. Not the piercing note of a Legion's horn. No, this was a harsh, lugubrious sound that set the lake's surface rippling and sent the birds screaming from the trees. A second horn joined in, echoed by two, then three more. The clarion cry sent a shiver of fear down Duvain's spine.

The Eirdkilrs had arrived.

Chapter Eleven

The ground shuddered beneath the tramping feet of the barbarians. The darkness disgorged them like a swarm of enormous ants rushing toward Saerheim. But the general's message had gotten it wrong: the Eirdkilrs numbered not in the hundreds, but the *thousands*.

Duvain clenched his fists, but found his hands shaking. He gripped his shield tighter and hoped no one noticed.

"Steady, lads." Corporal Rold spoke from nearby, his voice soft. His presence was solid, reliable at Duvain's back. Gone was the mockery, the disdain, the harshness from his voice. He spoke to keep them in line, stand strong against the enemy. "Pucker factor may be a ten out of ten, but that's no excuse to piss yourselves. Clench tight, and keep your eyes and steel forward."

Duvain almost found himself laughing in hysteric fear. Panic gripped him with a hand of ice, and only the solid feel of his weapons and the cold voice of the corporal kept him from emptying his bladder.

The barbarians' rush slowed, and they drew up in a ragged line a short distance from Saerheim.

"What're they doing?" Duvain whispered to Owen.

"Keeping out of bowshot," the private whispered back. His voice shook—he was as terrified as Duvain. "They know what our ballistae can do to them."

Duvain turned to Owen with a confused expression. "But we don't have ballistae."

Owen nodded. "I know. And the moment they realize that, we're doomed."

Long minutes passed, and the mass of Eirdkilrs thickened as more and more came around the lake to join the ranks, until they became a solid black mass brightened sporadically by torches. The Eirdkilrs' chant carried the short distance to the palisade wall. Duvain didn't understand the words, but the meaning was clear. They called for blood.

"Shite!" Rold cursed. Duvain followed his gaze. A small contingent of men had broken away from the mass, advancing toward the gate at a steady pace. They walked slowly, their steps hesitant. They no doubt expected to be scythed down by the massive ballistae bolts.

No bolts came. The Deadheads had no artillery.

The Eirdkilrs drew within forty paces of the gate and stopped at the base of the steep hill. They crouched behind a low farm wall, their gazes searching the ramparts. Duvain felt their gazes pause on him, and ice ran down his spine. From this distance, he imagined his death written in their eyes.

After a few moments, the Eirdkilrs stood and spread their arms wide. A few shouted in a derisive tone, and one dropped his leather breeches to expose his naked rear to the ramparts. This sent a ripple of laughter through the mass of waiting barbarians.

Still no response from Saerheim. With a shout, the throng of barbarians began to move forward, surging up the hill.

"Keeper have mercy," Rold muttered. "There's no stopping them now."

Duvain's chest tightened at the grim tone in the corporal's voice. Rold's face had gone pale. Weasel's eyes were closed, and his lips formed silent words. Was he praying?

Duvain sought out Endyn near the gate. His brother was lucky. On the ground, he couldn't see the wall of barbarians approaching. He didn't have to see his death drawing closer one lumbering step at a time.

A lone howl rose from the mass of Eirdkilrs. Another voice added to the keening cry. More and more joined in, until thousands of throats shouted their rage into the darkness. The cry died slowly, the sound seeming to echo from all around them.

The Eirdkilrs charged.

"Brace yourselves!" Rold shouted. "Here they come!"

The barbarians raced toward them, leaping walls, their booted feet trampling the few plants remaining on the barren farmland. Up the hill the Eirdkilrs came, thousands of massive, fur-covered brutes wielding huge axes, heavy war clubs, and spears nearly twice the length of a man. Moonlight glinted off their helmets—not the horned decorative headpieces of legend, but skull caps that looked all the more ominous for the simplicity. Wooden shields rode on their backs, and long knives hung like wolves' teeth from their belts.

"Ware arrows!" a voice shouted. Rold's, Duvain realized in the back of his mind.

He blinked. The men around him had crouched, but his body refused to heed his commands.

"Get down, you idiot!" A strong hand seized his collar and dragged him to the wooden ramparts. Something whizzed past his ear, narrowly missing slicing a furrow across the side of his head. Arrows *thunked* into the walls, *thumped* into the soft earth behind them, and, in the case of one unlucky Legionnaire, carved through flesh with deadly precision. The man went down with a scream, arrow embedded in his thigh.

Wide-eyed, Duvain looked at the man that had dragged him down. "Th-Thank you, Corporal," he stammered.

"Brick-headed, mouth-breathing numpty!" Rold scowled. "You're going to get yourself killed unless you wake the bloody hell up."

"Y-Yes, Corporal." Duvain's mouth was suddenly dry, yet sweat poured down his back. His hands shook so hard he couldn't hold his shield.

Rold seized his collar and shook him. "Snap out of it, meat! Stay focused or get dead."

The jostling shook something loose in Duvain's brain, and he found his mind and body back in harmony. He crouched with the other Legionnaires as the arrows rained down around them or slammed into the palisade wall. The tremor in his hand lessened as he forced himself to take deep breaths.

The rain of arrows diminished, replaced by the cries of the onrushing Eirdkilrs.

"Now, *up*!" Rold roared. He stood, the rest of the Legionnaires moving with him. "Loose hand axes!"

Duvain fumbled to draw the Fehlan weapon. He'd never even hit the target during the hours of practice he'd gotten in since arriving at Saerheim, but that didn't matter here. He had a sea of targets to choose from. The Eirdkilrs racing up the narrow wagon path clustered so tightly together he was assured to hit something. *Someone.*

He hurled his axe with the rest of the Legionnaires. The steel head flashed once in the torchlight and disappeared in the darkness. The war cries of the Eirdkilrs mingled with shouts of pain.

The command came again. "Loose second axe!"

Duvain's muscles moved slowly. His arm seemed to take an age to come up, back, and forward. The haft of the throwing axe slipped from his sweat-slicked palms. He didn't know if it hit anything, but had no time to think about it. Someone shoved him aside, and an arrow sliced through the air where he'd been standing a moment before.

Rold slapped him hard. "Eyes open, meat! Get ready to repel them!"

Duvain turned back to the wall and found the barbarians had closed the distance to the palisade. The Eirdkilrs didn't bother to use their shields—they simply charged the walls heedless of the risk of death. Among the chaotic mess of men, a few of the huge figures bore crude ladders, which were brought forward and quickly thrown up.

"Push 'em back!" Corporal Rold screamed. "Don't let them get over the wall!"

A ladder slammed onto the wall just beside Duvain, and he reached forward to shove it away. The heavy wood refused to budge. Lowering his shield, he used both hands to push. Weasel seized the ladder's other rail, and together they hurled it away.

Another ladder *clanked* on the wall, this time on Duvain's opposite side. By the time he had turned toward it, a wild, bearded face appeared over the edge of the wall. Owen drove his spear into the man's open mouth. Blood sprayed over Duvain's face, and the barbarian fell backward. With a shove, Owen sent the ladder after him.

The clash of steel melded with the cries of men, the Eirdkilrs' maddened howls, and a deep *thump, thump.* Duvain spared a glance for Endyn. His brother was hurled backward by the gate creaking inward. Endyn recovered his balance and threw himself against the huge doors, only to be thrown back again as the barbarians drove a battering ram against the gate.

"Push them back!" Rold was calling over the din of battle. "Keep the Watcher-damned bastards *off* the wall!" He punctuated his words by thrusting his spear into a barbarian's throat. The Eirdkilr's howl was cut off with a gurgle, and he fell back. A moment later, another barbarian replaced him on the ladder. When Weasel hacked him down, another man came.

And so it went for an eternity. The Legionnaires cut down as many as they could, but still the Eirdkilrs came on. The blood-curdling war cries continued, a wailing that pierced the clash of steel on steel. The sound grated on Duvain's ears. He fought back the instinctive fear and tried to focus on the task at hand.

Suddenly, without warning, there were no more. Duvain stumbled and fell to one knee. He found himself gasping for air. Fire consumed his arms and shoulders, and his forearms ached from gripping his spear and shield. Blood covered his arms, ran down his clothing, stained his face, leaked into his nose and mouth. How many Eirdkilrs had he killed? Had he killed any? He couldn't know for certain; it all faded into a crimson blur.

"Meat, you wounded?" someone shouted at him.

Duvain blinked. Corporal Rold hovered over him, his face spattered with gore, his expression concerned.

"I…" He found himself at a loss for words. He wanted to say he was fine, he wasn't wounded.

"You're bleeding," Rold told him.

Duvain looked down, and his brow furrowed. A gash ran from his left elbow to his shoulder, but he felt no pain. He felt nothing but the bone-numbing terror of battle.

"Damn, meat!" Rold shook his head. "If you don't get that stitched up, you'll bleed out."

As the fog of battle retreated, the pain asserted itself. A throbbing ache ran to his shoulder. His left hand felt weak as he gripped his shield.

"Owen, get meat here to the healer, double time!" Rold shouted.

Owen sat on the parapet, his back against the wooden wall. He had his eyes closed, his lips pressed in a tight line, as if fighting to keep down his meal.

"Private!" Rold gripped Owen's collar and dragged the man to his feet. "Do you hear me, soldier?"

"Yes, Corporal," Owen managed to mutter. His eyes opened, and he paled at the sight of Rold's bloodstained face.

Rold shoved Owen toward Duvain. "Get him to the healer, now!"

Owen moved as if in a trance, reaching for Duvain and helping him to stand. Duvain winced at the pain in his arm; with the fog of battle retreating, he was fully aware of its presence now. He needed Owen's help to climb down the ladder from the parapet.

He shot a glance at Endyn. His brother had a cut on his forehead and a mud stain on his knees, but otherwise looked unharmed.

"Corporal Rold!" Captain Lingram's voice cut through the night. "Status report." The captain strode toward them, his face a mask of concern.

Rold leapt from the parapet, landing on the ground beside Duvain, and pushed through the Legionnaires to meet the captain a short distance away. "Situation's dire, sir." He spoke in a voice too low for the men on the wall to hear, but Duvain caught everything as he limped past. "We've no hope of holding. We can stall them, but..."

"Understood." The captain nodded. "How long do we have?"

Rold shrugged. "They took a beating in that first round, so they'll retreat for a few minutes to lick their wounds before trying again. But they'll be back on us in five, ten minutes at most."

Captain Lingram's face hardened. "Then we've got to make use of the time."

Rold's face went blank. "Orders, Captain?"

Duvain slowed further. The fate of the Deadheads rested on Captain Lingram's next words.

The captain drew in a deep breath. "We've got to get as many of the villagers out of here as we can. Lord Virinus and his entourage as well. I want your squad heading up the flight."

"*My* squad?" Rold asked. "With respect, sir, the big one's our best hope of holding the gate as long as possible. Squad Three may not be the Legion's finest, but—"

"Corporal, you have your orders." Captain Lingram's voice brooked no dissent. "Get your men to the wagons and get the people moving."

"And you, sir?" Rold asked.

"I'll be commanding the rear guard, buying the rest of you time to escape."

"Not a bloody chance." A new voice entered the discussion: Sergeant Brash's. "You can stuff that order up your arse, with all due respect, sir."

Duvain stopped, unable to help himself listening to the debate.

Captain Lingram's expression grew angry. "Sergeant, while I appreciate—"

"Appreciate *nothing,* sir." The sergeant spoke in his cold, quiet voice. "You know as well as I do that *you're* the best chance of any of us making it back to Icespire in one piece. You know the terrain better than any of us, and you're one of the few that speaks enough Fehlan to communicate with the villagers. That makes you the best man to head up the retreat party."

"He's right, Captain." Awr had joined the debate now. "And you know it. It's just your Keeper-damned pride and loyalty that's talking you into staying. We both know how that'd turn out."

Captain Lingram's face hardened. "I thought my soldiers had more respect than this."

"We've all the respect in the world, Captain," Brash replied. "Which is why we're all going to tell you that we'll knock you out cold and tie you to the wagons before we let you command the rear guard."

Captain Lingram's eyes narrowed. "You speak of mutiny, Sergeant."

"Call it what you will, captain." Brash shrugged. "Whatever it takes to get you out of here in one piece."

"Damn it, Brash, I won't stand by and let you do this!" Captain Lingram's voice rose to a shout.

"Begging your pardon, sir, but I'm not giving you much choice." Brash folded his arms over his chest. "After what you did for me in Garrow's Canyon, I owe you. Seems like as fine a time as any to make good on that debt."

Captain Lingram tried to speak, but Awr cut him off, "You've a part to play in all this, Captain. You've got to get the *Fjall* chieftain's

148

daughter back to Icespire and make sure that treaty gets signed. Would you really trust Lord Virinus with command of your men?"

The captain's brow furrowed.

"He'd get everyone killed before daybreak." Awr shook his head. "The rest of them are counting on you, sir." He saluted. "Brash and I'll mind the village in your absence. Might even have a nice warm meal prepared for you when you get back."

Captain Lingram tried to speak, but no words came. He swallowed and tried again. "How many can you spare?"

Sergeant Brash turned back to study the walls. "With thirty-five, I can hold long enough for you to get out."

Awr nodded. "We'll keep them busy for you, Captain."

Captain Lingram's eyes narrowed. "Awr, you don't have to do this. There's no debt between us."

"That's where you're wrong, sir." Awr gestured to his throat. "The bastards would've finished the job if it weren't for you. It cost you everything to stand up to that cunt Virinus for me. Not a day's gone by that I want to tell you to take it back, to sit down and let them hang me for thievery. You wouldn't be in this mess if it weren't for me."

"I did what was *right,* Awr. You were trying to feed your family. You didn't deserve—"

"And that *right* is what got you sent here in the first place." The corporal folded his arms. "I won't let your pig-headed insistence on being a good man get you killed."

Sergeant Brash and Corporal Awr straightened and gave Captain Lingram a solemn salute. "It was an honor, sir," Brash said.

The captain returned the salute with a hard expression. "Make the bastards pay, Sergeant."

"Aye, sir." Sergeant Brash nodded. He turned to Awr and clapped the corporal on the back. "Seems like a nice night to dance with the Long Keeper, doesn't it, Corporal?"

"That it does, Sergeant." Awr returned the grin. "And I've got my dance shoes all polished and ready for the party." With a nod to the captain, he turned and strode with Brash toward the east gate.

Captain Lingram watched them go, unable to take his eyes from them. When he finally turned away, tears glimmered in his eyes.

Duvain set off without a word. The captain deserved a moment alone.

"They're staying to die," Owen whispered.

Duvain nodded. "Die like Legionnaires." It was as much as anyone in the Legion of Heroes could ask for.

The villagers bustled about the town square, under the shouted commands of one of the other sergeants. Duvain stumbled through the mess of men and into the main longhouse where Eira had set up her makeshift infirmary.

One of the young women assisting the healer directed Duvain to take a seat. After a quick glance at his arm, she rattled off a question in Fehlan and held up a needle and catgut thread. Duvain nodded. The woman scurried away, returning a moment later with a bowl of water and a cloth. She bathed the wound, eliciting a wince from Duvain, and set about stitching it up. Duvain gritted his teeth against the pain and bit back a cry. So many of the others were far worse off than he; it would dishonor their suffering if he cried out.

Four men lay silent on the pallets, eyes wide and unseeing. Another Legionnaire screamed as Eira wrestled with the shaft of an arrow buried in his gut. Blood pumped from two more arrows in his thigh and shoulder. His cries grew weaker as the pool of crimson around him widened, until he fell unconscious. The healer cursed in Fehlan and moved on to the next Legionnaire.

The young woman said something in Fehlan, gathered up her bowl, and left. Duvain studied his arm—the stitching was crude, but at least the wound would heal. He'd bear a nasty scar for the rest of his life. He'd be lucky to get away with *just* a scar.

The smell of death hung thick in the longhouse. The metallic tang of blood mixed with the stench of loosening bowels, accentuated by the pungent aroma of Eira's potions, poultices, and salves. Smoke from the fire burning in the earthen pit filled the enclosed space.

Duvain's brow furrowed. No, that couldn't be right. The few embers in the firepit emitted little smoke and no heat. The smell of burning straw came a moment later. He glanced at the roof, and his eyes went wide at the sight. The wooden ceiling beams and dry thatch of the longhouse were ablaze.

"Get out!" he shouted at the top of his lungs. "Fire!"

Eira turned to him, and he pointed upward. "Fire!" he shouted again.

The healer followed his finger, her eyes widening at the sight of the burning roof. Without hesitation, she barked orders to her assistants, and they scrambled to finish tying the dressings on the two Legionnaires they tended. Duvain raced toward the nearest wounded, a Legionnaire with his arm in a sling and a bandage around his head.

"Can you stand?" he shouted.

The man fixed him with a blank stare.

"The longhouse is burning!" Duvain reached for the man's good arm and tried to help him stand.

The Legionnaire stared dumbly at him, fresh blood staining the bandage on his head.

"Owen!" Duvain shouted. "Owen!"

Owen appeared a moment later. His face turned a nauseated green at the sight of so much blood, but Duvain's shouts drew his attention.

"We have to get them out of here before the longhouse burns down!"

Nodding, Owen stooped to help another wounded Legionnaire to stand.

Duvain half-dragged, half-carried the man outside the longhouse. Horror thrummed through him at the sight that greeted him.

Saerheim burned.

Fire consumed the thatched roofs of the longhouses. Smoke hung thick in the air, setting him coughing. The Legionnaire beside him grunted, and the weight on Duvain's shoulder suddenly lessened. He whirled, wide-eyed. The man lay on his back, a flaming arrow buried in his chest.

"Duvain!" A thick voice echoed above the *crackle* of flames. "Duvain!"

Duvain recognized the voice. "Endyn!" he shouted. "Over here."

A massive figure lumbered through the choking grey clouds. Endyn's face creased into a relieved smile. "We need to get out of here!" he shouted.

"I know, but we can't leave the wounded." Duvain turned back to the main longhouse. Owen had a wounded man's arm slung over his shoulder. A moment later, Eira appeared at the door, supporting another Legionnaire.

Duvain rushed past them and into the longhouse. Smoke, so thick Duvain could hardly see, set him coughing. A terrible heat filled the air, constricting his lungs. His eyes scanned the murky haze for any sign of movement.

His foot struck something hard and he stumbled, falling forward. He cried out as pain raced up his injured arm. Looking down, he glimpsed a body through the smoke. One of the healer's assistants. She wasn't moving.

With his good hand, Duvain grasped her collar and dragged her toward the door. Soot filled his lungs, setting him coughing. The heat in the longhouse intensified as the fire spread down the walls. A wooden beam collapsed not five paces from his head, and another crashed to the ground somewhere in the back of the smoke-filled longhouse. The building crumbled around him, but he couldn't drag the unconscious woman any faster.

Endyn's bulk materialized beside him. He bent, lifted the woman, and slung her over his shoulder. "Let's go!" he shouted.

Duvain stumbled after him out into the night. A heartbeat after he staggered through the open door, the longhouse's central beam *crashed* to the ground. The roof collapsed, bringing down the walls with a thunderous roar. Dust and smoke billowed around them.

"This way!" Endyn cried.

Duvain rushed after his brother. Outside, the wind kept the smoke at bay enough that they could see their way. The light of the burning village illuminated the outlines of the people rushing toward the west gate. Women, children, and the aged huddled just within the gate, surrounded by the thirty remaining Legionnaires. Captain Lingram, Lord Virinus, and the four mercenaries were there as well. Two of the mercenaries gripped a hastily-improvised litter, upon which lay the small form of a girl. Branda, daughter of Eirik Throrsson.

The men of Saerheim, however, marched in the *opposite* direction—toward the east gate and the Eirdkilrs waiting there. Their faces were grim, set in hard expressions. Duvain read it in their eyes: they knew their pitchforks, scythes, and rusted weapons couldn't hope to match the Eirdkilrs' weapons, but they would fight to give their families a chance to escape.

"Soldier, is that the last of the wounded?" Captain Lingram shouted at Endyn.

Endyn hesitated. "The longhouse collapsed."

"We got out the ones we could, Captain," Duvain answered.

Captain Lingram's brow furrowed, but he nodded. "That's all anyone could ask for."

"Captain, if we are to make our escape, we must move *now!*" Lord Virinus snapped. "Nothing matters more than the safety of the *Hilmir's* daughter."

The captain nodded. "I understand, my lord. I have no desire to hesitate any longer than necessary, but the retreat must be coordinated."

Lord Virinus drew himself up to his full, less-than-impressive height. "I command you to—"

Captain Lingram rounded on him, his eyes flashing hotter than the burning village. "You surrendered your right to command, my lord. Until we are safely back in Icespire, *I* am in charge here. Do not forget it."

Lord Virinus bristled, but Captain Lingram's glare silenced him.

Expression sorrowful, Captain Lingram glanced toward the east side of the camp, where the Legionnaires and villagers fought to buy them time to escape. Clearly he wanted to be with them, but he knew his duty lay in protecting the villagers, Lord Virinus' company, and his men still alive. With a sad shake of his head, he turned back to the people assembled at the gate.

"All right, lads," he said in a quiet voice, "it's time to go."

Chapter Twelve

Duvain forced himself to take slow, steady breaths. The fear roiling in his stomach threatened to overwhelm him. Judging by the nervous shifting of the men beside him, dismay held them all in its icy grip.

Thirty Legionnaires formed the shield wall—three ranks deep, and ten men long—barely enough to span the broad gate. Duvain had no doubt the Eirdkilrs would overrun them easily, but Captain Lingram's orders had been clear. They *had* to stand. It was the only way the villagers would escape.

It took three hundred people a surprising amount of time to leave. Two heavily-laden wagons had evacuated the soldiers too wounded to stand, along with enough supplies for the journey to Sentry Garrison. The villagers had left behind everything they couldn't carry—their entire lives' work burned in their longhouses, but they had no choice but to flee.

If only they'd flee faster! Close to fifty villagers crowded toward the gate, waiting for their turn to leave. The exodus could only have taken ten minutes, but to Duvain, it felt like a lifetime.

The cries of the Legionnaires holding the east gate drifted through the crackling of the burning longhouses. Every sound pierced Duvain's heart. He knew what was happening at the gate. Sergeant Brash, Corporal Awr, and their Legionnaires fought beside the men of Saerheim to give them a chance to survive. They faced Eirdkilrs in the thousands, and they numbered fewer than forty. It was only a matter of time.

Time ran out sooner than Duvain expected. Huge figures appeared in the smoke, racing around the village, filling the night with bestial war cries. Two, three, five, six. Six Eirdkilrs, massive men with beards as shaggy as the Wasteland ice bear pelts they wore. They gripped massive war clubs, axes, and spears far too heavy for any but the strongest Legionnaire to lift. Duvain had no desire to see the carnage those weapons could wreak. He gritted his teeth and whispered a silent prayer to the Swordsman that the barbarians would be too busy with the burning houses to notice them.

Icy blue Eirdkilr eyes came to rest on the line of Legionnaires, and vicious grins split their huge faces. Howling into the sky, they hefted their weapons and charged. Their long legs ate up the ground at an impossible pace—or maybe it was just Duvain's fear that sped everything up. His mouth went dry, and his arms refused to respond to his commands to raise his shield.

The pack of Eirdkilrs crashed into the shield wall with bone-jarring force. The front rank of Legionnaires stumbled back, and a shield rim slammed into Duvain's face. Blood filled his mouth. The taste snapped him from his stupor. Lifting his spear, he thrust it toward the barbarian pressing against the Legionnaire to his right. The spear head struck a glancing blow, bouncing off the thick, white hides slung over the barbarian's back. With a wild cry, the Eirdkilr raised his axe and brought it smashing down onto a stocky Legionnaire in the front row. The man— Duvain didn't know his name— barely managed to raise his shield to block the blow. He cried out as the impact shattered his arm and drove him to one knee.

Duvain struck again, and this time the spear found its target. The blade cut a long gash across the barbarian's cheek. The Eirdkilr whirled toward him and unleashed a war cry, raising his axe to strike. Another Legionnaire brought the savage down with the thrust of a short sword into his gut. When the Eirdkilr fell to his knees, the same soldier tore out his throat with the edge of his blade.

Something big and heavy slammed into Duvain's left side. He turned and raised his sword to defend himself, but it was only Endyn. His brother had been knocked into him by the Legionnaire in front of him. The soldier in the front row fell without a scream, an Eirdkilr axe splitting him from crown to shoulder. The barbarian released his grip on the heavy battle axe and drew his sword. Endyn's hewing spear removed his head in one great, sweeping motion. The barbarian's decapitated body fell backward, spraying blood.

The sudden rush of battle faded as the last Eirdkilr fell beneath the stabbing Legionnaire short swords. Duvain stared wildly around, unable to believe it. They'd survived!

Not all of them. Four Legionnaires had fallen to the Eirdkilrs, and two more were too badly wounded to keep fighting.

"Legionnaires, fall back!"

The cry came from the gate. Captain Lingram stood there, beckoning for them. The gate was clear, and the retreating backs of the fleeing villagers could be seen disappearing into the darkness.

"Double time!" Corporal Rold shouted. Wiping blood—his own, and that of the man who'd died beside him—from his eyes, he reached for one of the wounded Legionnaires and helped him up. "Let's go, soldier!"

"My arm!" the man screamed. His sword arm ended just below the shoulder; the rest lay on the ground.

"We'll get you a new one, soldier!" Rold snapped. "For now, we run."

The man's cries of agony grew louder as he stumbled after Rold. Duvain found himself rooted to the spot. He couldn't flee—his feet refused to heed his commands to move. He couldn't tear his eyes from the lifeless bodies around him. Eirdkilr lay beside Legionnaire, each equally silent and motionless in death.

"Duvain!" Endyn's cry filtered through the blood pounding in his ears. "Let's go!"

Duvain moved, slowly, as if lead filled his legs, stumbling after his retreating company.

Beside the gate, a third wagon waited for the wounded soldiers. The driver fought for control of his horse, which reared and plunged, its eyes wide. The smell of blood and smoke drove it wild with fear.

The beast let out a terrified shriek and reared once more. It took Duvain's mind a moment to register the arrow that had suddenly sprouted from the horse's neck. Beside him, the driver fell with a cough, hurled to the side by an invisible hand. He lay where he'd fallen, blood trickling from the arrow lodged in his throat.

"Enemy contact!" Rold shouted. "About face, lads!"

The corporal seized Duvain's arm and whirled him about. At the far end of the main square, a few hundred paces away, dozens of Eirdkilrs appeared through the smoke. Ten of them carried bows, which they drew back and loosed at the huddled Legionnaires. Duvain ducked behind his shield as the arrows *thunked* into the earth around him.

"The gates!" Captain Lingram shouted. "Get to the gates!"

Duvain watched from behind his shield as Weasel, Owen, and two other Legionnaires rushed toward the open gate. He knew it would be futile—the Eirdkilrs would swarm over them in a matter of minutes.

A looming figure lumbered past him. Endyn. His brother raced not toward the gate, but in the direction of the cart. The horse's protests had quieted, its struggles weakening as the blood gushed from the arrow wound in its neck. With a quiet moan, it fell and lay still.

"Endyn, what are you doing?" Duvain screamed.

"Help me!" Endyn cried. Drawing his sword, he cut the horse's traces and seized the cart's wheels.

Duvain suddenly understood. Closing the gate would do little, but Endyn had found a way to *block* them.

He raced toward Endyn. "Owen!" he cried, thrusting a finger toward the nearest burning home. "Get fire."

With a nod, Owen raced off.

The barbarians' howls of delight filled the night, adding to the clatter of arrows *thumping* into the earth around Duvain, Endyn, and Weasel. Endyn heaved on the wagon, dragging it toward the gate.

"Corporal, we need to get the wounded out of here!" Duvain shouted. "We'll hold them off, at least a little while."

Rold's jaw had taken on a stubborn set. "You're idiots if you think this'll work."

Duvain ignored him. He reached the wagon and gripped one of the shafts, lending his weight and strength to Endyn's. Weasel did the same with the other shaft.

The wagon, loaded with provisions, weighed more than Duvain had expected. Even after Rold got the wounded off the wagon and on their feet, the three of them struggled to move it even a hand's breadth. He cast a glance back and his heart sank. The horse's struggles had cracked the front axle.

But that didn't stop him from pulling for all he was worth. They had to cover the escape, no matter what. If they didn't, Awr, Brash, and the other Legionnaires at the east gate would have sacrificed their lives for nothing.

The approaching Eirdkilrs seemed to understand what they were doing. Arrows whistled down around the three of them, and Endyn grunted as one *pinged* off his breastplate. Duvain ducked into the protective cover of the wagon.

Weasel moved too slowly. He shrieked and fell, an arrow piercing his leg. Without a shield, he couldn't protect himself from the arrows. Howling in pain, he crawled under the wagon.

Endyn cried out. Duvain's eyes widened—an arrow protruded from the side of his breastplate. A moment later, another *thunked* into his upper shoulder, followed by another in his leg. But the big Legionnaire refused to fall. With a grimace, he leaned forward and dragged the wagon onward.

Duvain had a choice: help Endyn or shield him from the arrows. It was no choice at all. Releasing his grip on the wagon, he dove for a fallen Legionnaire's shield and raced around Endyn. He took up position between his brother and the oncoming barbarians. Arrows *thumped* into the shield as Duvain tried to block the incoming shafts.

Too many slipped past. Every time Duvain looked back, a new shaft had pierced Endyn's chest, shoulder, back, sides, and legs. The barbarians loosed as they raced toward the struggling Legionnaires. Within seconds, Duvain knew they'd be overwhelmed.

"Endyn!" he screamed.

With a cry, Endyn threw his weight into dragging the wagon. The wheels creaked forward for a moment before, with an ominous *crack,* the axle snapped. The wagon tilted precariously—right toward the open gate. Duvain shielded Endyn as his brother raced around to the side of the wagon, crouched, pressed his shoulder against the underside of the wagon, and heaved. His muscles corded, his huge legs driving upward. A thunderous roar rumbled from his throat. Slowly, the wagon wheels lifted from the ground, and it toppled over onto its side with a tremendous *crash.*

Endyn sagged, exhausted. The effort had taken everything out of him.

"Get over the wagon!" Duvain shouted.

Endyn struggled to his feet and tried to scramble up onto the wagon bed. His arms trembled, exhausted from the effort, and he fell.

Duvain's gaze darted toward the oncoming Eirdkilrs. They had reached the well, and closed the remaining distance to the gate at full speed. Their howling war cries grew louder as they drew closer.

A small figure appeared from the thick smoke. Owen raced toward them, a torch held in his hands.

Duvain's gut tightened. The Eirdkilrs spotted the racing Legionnaire, and their bows turned toward him. More than a dozen barbarians loosed at the same time. The shafts streaked through the darkness toward Owen.

The first took him in the leg, just above the knee. The second punched into his side, followed by two more. He fell hard, and the rest whistled over his head. He crawled toward them, keening a cry of agony.

Before Duvain realized what was happening, Endyn had pushed past him and raced toward the fallen Legionnaire.

"Endyn, no!" Duvain shouted.

His brother, heedless of his warning, crossed the distance to Owen in five great steps, reached down, and lifted the man into his arms. He whirled, shielding Owen's body with his own. Arrows pelted all around him, more than a few slamming into him, sending him staggering. He crashed into the wagon and fell hard, but staggered up again. He lifted Owen high and passed him into the waiting arms beyond. Somehow, the Legionnaire stubbornly clung to his torch, as if clutching a shield to ward off enemy arrows.

He turned to Duvain. "You're next!" Without waiting, he lifted Duvain, armor and all, and propelled him over the wagon. Duvain crashed to the ground. The impact knocked the wind from his lungs. Ignoring the ache, he leapt to his feet and spun toward the cart.

Endyn's massive figure appeared over the wagon, a mountain illuminated by the village burning behind him. Something slammed into his back, knocking him forward. He fell hard and landed face-first in the churned mud. He didn't move.

"No!" In horror, Duvain stared down at his brother. More than twenty shafts protruded from Endyn's back, neck, and legs. Some of the broad-headed arrows had punched through his breastplate, mail shirt, and gambeson.

He crouched over his brother. "Damn you, Endyn, get up!"

His brother didn't respond.

"Endyn!" Tears streamed down his cheeks, and sorrow thickened his throat. He shook his brother. "Don't do this to me, curse you."

Strong hands gripped him and dragged him away. "Meat!" Corporal Rold shouted in his ear. "We've got to move."

Duvain fought to free himself. He couldn't leave Endyn, not like this…

"Damn it, Duvain!" Corporal Rold tackled him, bringing him down to the muddy ground. "Your brother's gone, soldier." The corporal's voice was harsh in Duvain's ear. "And we'll all join him if we don't get out of here."

Duvain screamed and shouted, but the corporal held him fast.

"Corporal," a weak voice cut through the din. Owen, lying on the ground, held up the torch. "The wagon." He coughed, bringing up blood. "Fire…the wagon."

The momentary distraction gave Duvain the chance he needed to break free. He squirmed out from under Corporal Rold, staggered to his feet, and snatched the torch from Owen's hand.

As Duvain reached the wagon, the face of a massive Eirdkilr loomed over the side. Howling a cry of delight, the barbarian raised his massive club to crush Duvain's skull. Terror froze Duvain. The torch in his hand hovered just short of a bale of straw that lay abandoned next to the wagon.

A throwing axe hurtled past Duvain's head, burying deep in the Eirdkilr's face. The savage's delight turned to agony. Blood sprayed, and the huge barbarian toppled backward.

Corporal Rold appeared beside Duvain, sword in hand. "Do it, damn you!"

Duvain threw the torch into the pile of straw. The flame licked eagerly at the dry strands and, within moments, the wood was ablaze. The clash of steel echoed just beside Duvain's head. Another Eirdkilr had climbed onto the overturned wagon, only to be cut down by Corporal Rold. Another Legionnaire battled a second barbarian beyond.

As Duvain turned away, he caught a familiar hand poking out from beneath the wagon. The long, slim fingers, still gripping the sword, could only belong to Weasel. Blood soaked the ground around the body, now riddled with arrows. He turned away, not wanting to watch the fire consume the corpse of his comrade. His friend.

The lump returned to Duvain's throat as his eyes went to Endyn's body. With the last of his strength, he willed his brother to move, to stir, to breathe. Nothing happened. His brother hadn't moved. With all those arrows in him, he *wouldn't* move again.

"Let's go, soldier!" Corporal Rold gripped his arm and dragged him away. "We've got minutes before they find a way past."

Duvain didn't protest. He followed, his limbs numb, his mind blank. Only the corporal's hand on his arm kept him moving, kept him from collapsing. His mind refused to comprehend what had just happened. His world had shattered with his brother's death.

He cast a final glance back. The light of the burning wagon cast a funereal glow on Endyn's body, so silent and still.

Wait, was that—?

It was!

Endyn's back rose and fell. He was breathing!

Duvain blinked. Was it just a cruel trick of his brain? No, it was real. Endyn blinked, and his head lifted slowly from the ground.

Eyes wide, Duvain watched, incredulous. He couldn't believe it.

"Help...me," Endyn rumbled.

The words pierced Duvain's shocked numbness. He ripped his arm from Rold's grasp and raced back toward his brother. "Endyn!"

"Damn it, meat, he—" Rold's cry cut off with a surprised gasp.

Duvain skidded to a halt beside Endyn. His brother struggled to rise to his elbows, groaning with the effort. Duvain hauled on Endyn's arm, helping him to his feet.

Rold appeared on Endyn's other side. "By the Keeper!" he breathed. "How in the bloody hell...?"

Duvain had no answer, but it didn't matter. All that mattered was that Endyn was *alive!* More than that, he was walking and talking, though pain rendered his voice tight.

Together, he and Rold helped Endyn limp down the hill and out of the light of the burning village. When they'd reached the shadows of the forest, Rold slipped out from beneath Endyn's arm.

"How in the bloody hell are you still alive?" he demanded.

Endyn glanced down at his body. "I-I don't know."

Duvain studied his brother. A few of the arrows had fallen loose in their struggle. Through the holes in the mail shirt and gambeson, Duvain caught a glimpse of the thick, grey scales.

"Impossible!" he gasped.

The scales had grown thicker since the last time he'd seen his brother's back. Blood trickled from small puncture wounds in the stony grey surface. The Eirdkilrs' arrows, driven by the force of their powerful bows, had punched through his breastplate, mail shirt, and gambeson. But the dragonskin had saved him.

Duvain tested the theory by tugging on another of the arrows. Though Endyn yelped, the arrowhead pulled loose of the mail shirt with little effort.

One by one, he tugged the arrows free, to the astonishment of the other Legionnaires around him. Thirty arrows had struck his brother—thirty arrows fell to the ground, leaving little more than small punctures to mark their passage.

"Watcher's beard!" one of the Legionnaires breathed. "It's a miracle!"

Rold lifted Endyn's shirt, revealing the thick, crusted scales on his back. "Not a miracle," he growled. "Bloody good fortune, I'd say."

The two arrows in Endyn's leg pulled free as well, though without armor to protect his lower body, the arrowheads had been driven in a bit deeper. None of the Legionnaires could believe it—Duvain struggled with it himself.

The dragonskin that had plagued Endyn for so many years had just saved his life? Impossible! Yet there was no mistake. Endyn had survived because of it.

Rold whistled. "If anyone'd told me that story, I'd have called him a madman." He shook his head. "You're one lucky bastard, you know that?"

A broad grin spread Endyn's massive face, and he colored, this time with pride instead of embarrassment.

The howling of the Eirdkilrs shattered the momentary calm. Their cries echoed with fury at being stymied in their attempts to capture the Legionnaires.

"Can you walk?" Rold asked Endyn.

Endyn nodded.

"Good," said the corporal, tightening his grip on his sword, "then we need to get the fiery hell out of here. It won't take long for them to find a way around. When they do, we'd better be as far away from here as possible."

Chapter Thirteen

A hundred fearful faces turned toward them, and relief shone in the eyes of the villagers as they recognized the Legionnaires. Captain Lingram pushed through the crowd of people and rushed toward them as they approached.

"Situation report, Corporal."

Corporal Rold gave a tired salute. "Saerheim has officially fallen, sir."

Captain Lingram's face grew pale. "Watcher have mercy," he said in a quiet voice, bowing his head.

"The bastards had overrun the village, and they'd have caught us if not for the big one." Rold inclined his head toward Endyn. "He blocked the gate, bought us a few minutes at least."

Captain Lingram turned to Endyn. "All of us owe our lives to you, soldier. You've done the Legion proud."

"Thank you, sir," Endyn rumbled. "But I didn't do it alone." He dropped his gaze to the body in his arms. Even after Owen had grown too weak to walk, Endyn had ignored Rold's orders and carried Owen all this way. He didn't care that the Legionnaire hadn't moved in half an hour. Duvain could see the weariness in Endyn's limbs and face, but his brother refused to leave Owen. "He…he was the real hero, sir. Weasel, too. Gave everything he had."

Sorrow filled Captain Lingram's eyes. "All of you are." He lifted his eyes to Duvain, Rold, and the six Legionnaires that had guarded the rear. "Each and every one. Your courage and loyalty will be rewarded when we reach Icespire."

Rold nodded. "Let's get on with that, then, sir. The more distance we put between us and those savages, the better I'll feel."

"I couldn't agree more." Lord Virinus' voice held the petulance of a spoiled child. He had joined them at the rear of the company. "It's a pity more of you didn't survive. We'll need every able-bodied man to reach Sentry Garrison ahead of the barbarians." He looked up at Endyn. "You, giant. Your friend is dead. Your strength is needed for the living."

Captain Lingram turned to Virinus, his jaw clenched. "My lord—"

Lord Virinus ignored the captain, but turned to the crowd. "Barcus, Scathan!" He called out. "Bring the girl here."

The mercenaries pushed through the crowd, gripping the makeshift stretcher carrying the chieftain's daughter.

Lord Virinus waved at Endyn. "Let *him* carry her. Your swords will be better served protecting us all." He turned a hard gaze on Captain Lingram. "Unless you can truly say your man is worth my *four* blades?"

Captain Lingram's eyes narrowed and his mouth opened.

"Captain," Endyn rumbled, cutting off whatever he'd been about to say. "I will carry her. But give me a moment." He lifted Owen's body. "He deserves to be set to rest."

After a moment of hesitation, Captain Lingram nodded.

Endyn disappeared into the woods, Owen's body cradled in his huge arms. Duvain wanted to go with him, but the look in Endyn's face held him back. When he returned empty-handed a few minutes later, tears streaked his huge cheeks. Without a word, he lifted the girl from the stretcher. He strode toward the head of the line in silence.

"Thank you, my lord." Captain Lingram spoke through clenched teeth.

168

"For what?" Confusion stained the nobleman's face.

"For volunteering your men to join my company."

The nobleman's eyes went wide, but Captain Lingram turned away, addressing the four mercenaries. "You know these woods better than us. You will serve as the rear guard. Stay two hundred paces behind the main group. If the Eirdkilrs come, *do not* engage, but report to me at once. Understood?"

The mercenaries' eyes darted to Lord Virinus, whose face had gone a furious shade of purple. "How dare you command my men?" he railed. "You—"

"You said your men would be better protecting us all," Captain Lingram retorted, his voice hard. "I am simply doing as you said, *my lord.*" The last two words came out in a growl.

The nobleman's eyes narrowed. "You overstep yourself, Captain. These men are here to protect me, and—"

"Do you wish to live long enough to see Icespire?" Captain Lingram snarled. "If so, shut your mouth and follow my orders. Or by the Keeper, I'll string you up and leave you to the Eirdkilrs myself."

"You wouldn't dare!" Lord Virinus actually took a step back. "I am a nobleman of Icespire."

"And I am the commander of these men." The captain looked at the mercenaries. "*All* of them. Every one of us will be needed to survive. Even you, my lord. Now, get back to the head of the line and keep people moving." He dropped his voice. "Be useful, for once, Myron."

Virinus gaped, but no sound came out from his mouth.

Captain Lingram turned to the mercenaries. "Move out. Now!" His voice brooked no disobedience.

The mercenaries obeyed. Their mottled brown cloaks blended with the shadows of the forest as they returned down the road toward Saerheim, until Duvain lost sight of them in the darkness.

"As for the rest of you," Captain Lingram said to Duvain and the other Legionnaires, "bring up the rear, and be wary. We're counting on you to alert us if the Eirdkilrs catch up."

Despite his exhaustion, Duvain snapped a crisp salute. "Aye, sir." He adjusted his grip on his shield and spear and stood straighter.

With a nod, Captain Lingram strode away, leaving a gaping Lord Virinus.

Duvain and the other Legionnaires ignored the nobleman, but took their place at the rear of the line without a word. A moment later, Lord Virinus stormed past, muttering dark curses on Captain Lingram.

Duvain strained his ears, listening for any sign of pursuit. Dread grew heavy within him. Any minute now, the howling of the Eirdkilrs would split the night.

After the din of battle and the roaring fire, the sounds of night were oddly muted to Duvain. A night owl hooted high in a yew tree, while the chill wind filled the air with the rustling of dry autumn leaves. The clanking of the Legionnaire's armor seemed to echo from the forest around them, amplified by his anxiety. Boots squelched in mud. Children wailed for their beds and their fathers, only to be hushed by mothers who spoke in voices filled with sorrow. They would never see their men again, yet they marched on. Their children had to live.

Fear hung like a thick pall over them all. They all knew what pursued them, and that knowledge spurred them to move faster. The Eirdkilrs, unencumbered by belongings, children, and the aging, would eventually catch up, and the wave of death would sweep over them. They had every reason to move faster.

As they rounded a corner in the trail, Duvain caught a glimpse of the muddy patch of ground and fallen logs they'd passed on their way to the village. The Legionnaires gave the pile of logs a wide berth, herding the villagers into the forest to avoid pissing off the woodcutter vipers. Duvain shuddered at the memory of what lived there. Endyn had nearly died—he would have, had not the serpent's fangs struck the dragonskin. The dragonskin had saved him then, as it saved him back at Saerheim.

"Captain!" A voice pierced the tense silence of the night. Duvain's stomach twisted. It came from behind him.

He turned to see two of the mercenaries racing toward them, his eyes wide. "They're coming, Captain!" he cried. There was no sign of the other two.

Captain Lingram appeared at the rear of the train of people and animals. "How far?"

"They can't be more than five minutes out, sir!" the mercenary gasped, winded.

"Damn it!" Captain Lingram clenched his fists. He looked at the procession of people and soldiers—they had no way out. "We have to move faster!"

He shouted in Fehlan, and his words had an immediate effect. Women, children, and the village elders broke into a run, panic on their faces. The drivers of the two carts whipped the draft horses to move faster.

Duvain, Rold, and the other Legionnaires hustled after them. Duvain couldn't help looking over his shoulders. At any moment, the Eirdkilrs would appear around the bend in the road. He and his fellow Legionnaires would hold the rear in the hope that they could buy enough time for the rest to escape. A desperate hope, one with no chance of success.

As he cast a fearful glance back, his eyes fell on the pile of fallen logs. An idea struck him like a bolt of lightning. A dangerous, potentially suicidal idea. At this point, they had nothing else.

"Captain," he called. "Permission to remain in the rear?"

Captain Lingram shook his head. "Denied, soldier. This is neither the time nor place for a desperate last stand. We have to try to outrun them." His expression and the tone of his voice spoke volumes: he knew they had little hope, but he *had* to try.

"Captain, I've got an idea that could buy us a bit of time, but it'll only work if I'm the only one the Eirdkilrs see."

The captain's brow furrowed. "What are you thinking?"

Duvain explained his idea. The captain shook his head. "Not a chance!"

"It's the *only* chance, Captain," Duvain insisted. "It'll work—I know it. Get everyone off the road, into the forest. Keep moving north, toward Icespire. I'll catch up as soon as I can." He glanced toward Lord Virinus' mercenaries. "And I'll need someone to guide me."

One of the two mercenaries, the one named Scathan, stepped forward. "I'll go with him."

"So will I." Corporal Rold joined them.

Duvain shook his head. "Corporal, this isn't going to—"

"Get stuffed, meat." Corporal Rold replied, folding his arms. "I'll be damned if I let you have *all* the fun. Besides, someone's got to watch your back."

Duvain glanced up the road. He was glad Endyn had disappeared around a bend—he would have protested or insisted on coming along. He didn't want that. The plan was desperate and foolish, like as not to get him—and anyone who went with him—killed. But it would give Endyn a chance of survival.

The weeks spent marching and training had helped improve his brother's stamina. Though he was no doubt exhausted, he would keep going as long as he had to. And Duvain's plan might buy enough time for him to have a chance to reach safety.

Captain Lingram held out a hand. "Show them what a Legionnaire's made of, soldier."

Duvain gripped it. "It's been an honor, sir." He gave a salute, and the captain returned it. "One favor, Captain?"

The captain raised an eyebrow.

"Watch out for my brother, sir." A grin tugged at his lips, and he didn't try to fight it. "Mother'd have my head if anything happened to him."

The captain's smile matched his own. "I'll keep an eye on him, Legionnaire. But I'm sure your mother would want you to keep an eye on him yourself."

"I'll see what I can do, Captain."

Captain Lingram gripped Rold's hand, nodded to the mercenary, and rushed up the road after the retreating villagers.

Corporal Rold turned to Duvain with a derisive expression. "Time to hear this plan of yours, meat."

Duvain drew in a deep breath. "We're going to need torches."

* * *

Silence hung thick in the forest where the three of them crouched. The tension in Duvain's shoulders mounted with every passing second, knotting so tight he could barely move. He half-expected the barbarians to leap out from the trees and surround them. He forced himself to take deep breaths and keep his eyes fixed on the road that led toward Saerheim. The enemy would come from there.

Rold muttered in his ear. "If you get me killed, meat, I'm going to be *bloody* pissed!"

The corporal's words pushed back Duvain's fear a little. He shrugged. "Pull your head out of your ass, and you've a decent chance of survival."

Rold chuckled. "Hate to say it, but it turns out you're not the worst Legionnaire in the world."

"You're too kind," Duvain muttered. He was about to return Rold's insult, but his mouth went suddenly dry. Something moved in the dark. *Somethings.* Figures coalesced from the shadows, tens, scores, hundreds. Huge, bearded figures wearing white furs and carrying enormous war axes, clubs, and spears.

The Eirdkilrs had found them.

"You sure about this?" Rold asked.

Duvain shrugged. "Not even a little."

Drawing in a deep breath, Duvain stood and bellowed, "Hey, yak-buggers! Is it true you dye your faces because you're so ugly not even *you'd* fuck you?"

The Eirdkilrs whirled toward the sound of his voice, their eyes scanning the darkness for him.

He made it easy for them. "Here I am!" he shouted and raised the torch he'd kept hidden beneath a fallen tree. "Big fellas like you, it probably takes a whole search party to find a good idea among you. But how's this for encouragement?" He dropped his trousers and shook his arse at them.

The Eirdkilrs howled and raised their weapons high overhead. The sound of their cries chilled Duvain to the bone. He fumbled with the torch and nearly dropped it.

"Ugly fuckers, aren't you?" Corporal Rold sneered. "You lot have all the charm and charisma of a pile of burning dog shite."

Though the savages didn't understand the words, the tone was crystal clear. With a howl, they charged.

Duvain, Rold, and the mercenary turned and ran, holding their torches high overhead. The light illuminated their path through the forest and limned them clearly for the Eirdkilrs to see. Ululating cries filling the air, the mass of barbarians surged toward them.

Right through the muddy ground and over the fallen logs.

The first screams began a moment after a terrifying whirring pierced the night. Duvain cast one glance backward and shuddered. Dozens of barbarians raced onto the open, muddy field. The woodcutter vipers didn't welcome the intruders. Though Eirdkilrs wore thick furs on their backs, their leather breeches and boots proved no match for the serpents' powerful fangs. Men writhed on the ground, and the emerald green serpents slithered over them to bite at the next ranks.

Duvain threw his torch toward the fallen logs, and Rold and Scathan did likewise. Hundreds of woodcutters darted from holes in the ground, their scales whirring like a biting saw. The fire enraged the serpents further, sending them slithering toward the mass of barbarians. Eirdkilrs fell screaming. The crush of warriors prevented the foremost men from retreating. Many farther back died, trampled beneath their comrades' boots in their haste to flee the wrath of the vipers.

Rold's laughter followed Duvain through the night. "Well I'll be damned," the corporal muttered.

Duvain had no time for mirth. "You know where you're going?" he asked the mercenary.

The man nodded. "We'll lead them west a while, then cross the *Jokull* River and backtrack toward the road to rejoin the rest of the company. If all goes well, we'll meet up with them before midday."

Midday! Duvain stifled a groan. The fight and flight had drained him, and this last rush of adrenaline left him exhausted. He doubted he could run through the remaining hours before dawn. But what choice did he have? They *had* to lead the Eirdkilrs away from the rest of their company. It was the only way Endyn, Captain Lingram, and the others would survive. They had to get Branda to Sentry Garrison and keep her alive to cement the alliance with Eirik Throrsson and the *Fjall*. That was why the Deadheads had been sent to Saerheim, and he would be damned if he let a horde of barbarians make them fail.

He dropped his shield beside a tree, and left his armor a few paces away. Rold did the same. The Eirdkilrs couldn't miss a trail that visible. Besides, the heavy steel breastplate, mail shirt, and shield would only slow them down.

The night breeze grew suddenly chill, and he shivered. Alone, in the woods, with an army of Eirdkilrs behind them. Things didn't get direr than this.

But that was what the Legion did. They stood fast even in the most desperate situations. After all that had happened, he truly felt like he belonged. He was a Legionnaire. A Deadhead.

He turned to Rold with a grin. "It's a nice night for a stroll, isn't it, Corporal?"

Rold nodded. "That it is, meat. That it is."

With a sigh, Duvain turned and set off at a jog, following Scathan west. They had a long night ahead of them.

The End

The Adventures Aren't Over Yet!

There's still one final story to tell: the origin story of Captain Lingram, the Blacksword, and the only survivor of the fall of Highcliff Motte.

The Last March is the story of that battle, how a few brave souls gave all to keep an Eirdkilr horde at bay, though it cost them their lives.

The Last March

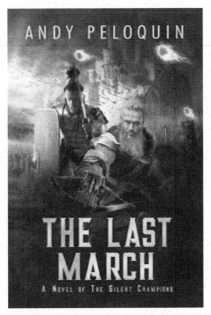

Sergeant Koltun and his Screaming Howlers should never have been caught up in the desperate battle to defend Highcliff Motte from a horde of Eirdkilrs. But with so few Legionnaires against so many barbarians, they couldn't simply ride away and leave their fellow soldiers to die.

Outnumbered, cut off from reinforcements, with no chance of victory, their only hope is to embark on one last march...every step a fight to survive.

The Last March is the sixth book in thrilling The Silent Champions military fantasy series, one final gritty novel to bring the battle full circle.

Fans of Malazan's Bridgeburners, 300, and The Black Company will love this dark, ominous tale of brave soldiers willing to give their all.

Enjoy More Series by Andy Peloquin

Plus, get backstory and insight into the epic world of Einan!

Queen of Thieves

Book 1: Child of the Night Guild

Book 2: Thief of the Night Guild

Book 3: Queen of the Night Guild

Traitors' Fate (**Queen of Thieves/Hero of Darkness Crossover**)

Hero of Darkness

Book 1: Darkblade Assassin

Book 2: Darkblade Outcast

Book 3: Darkblade Protector

Book 4: Darkblade Seeker

Book 5: Darkblade Slayer

Book 6: Darkblade Savior

Book 7: Darkblade Justice

Heirs of Destiny

Trial of Stone (Book 1)

Crucible of Fortune (Book 2)

Secrets of Blood (Book 3)

Storm of Chaos (Book 4)

Ascension of Death (Book 5)

The Renegade Apprentice (Book 6)

Different, Not Damaged: A Short Story Collection

About the Author

I am, first and foremost, a storyteller and an artist--words are my palette. Fantasy is my genre of choice, and I love to explore the darker side of human nature through the filter of fantasy heroes, villains, and everything in between. I'm also a freelance writer, a book lover, and a guy who just loves to meet new people and spend hours talking about my fascination for the worlds I encounter in the pages of fantasy novels.

Fantasy provides us with an escape, a way to forget about our mundane problems and step into worlds where anything is possible. It transcends age, gender, religion, race, or lifestyle--it is our way of believing what cannot be, delving into the unknowable, and discovering hidden truths about ourselves and our world in a brand new way. Fiction at its very best!

Join my Facebook Reader Group
for updates, LIVE readings, exclusive content, and all-around fantasy fun.
Let's Get Social!
Be My Friend: https://www.facebook.com/andrew.peloquin.1
Facebook Author Page: https://www.facebook.com/andyqpeloquin
Twitter: https://twitter.com/AndyPeloquin

Made in the USA
Coppell, TX
23 March 2020